The Glass Castle

Trisha White Priebe
& Jerry B. Jenkins

SHILOH RUN PRESS

An Imprint of Barbour Publishing, Inc.

© 2016 by Trisha White Priebe

Print ISBN 978-1-63409-389-7

eBook Editions:
Adobe Digital Edition (.epub) 978-1-63409-762-8
Kindle and MobiPocket Edition (.prc) 978-1-63409-763-5

All scripture quotations are taken from the King James Version of the Bible.

This book is a work of fiction. Names, characters, places, and incidents are either products of the author's imagination or used fictitiously. Any similarity to actual people, organizations, and/or events is purely coincidental.

Cover Illustration: Scott Altmann
Cover Lettering: Kirk DouPonce

Published in association with The Blythe Daniel Agency, P.O. Box 64197, Colorado Springs, CO 80962-4197.

Published by Shiloh Run Press, an imprint of Barbour Publishing, Inc., P.O. Box 719, Uhrichsville, Ohio 44683, www.shilohrunpress.com

Our mission is to publish and distribute inspirational products offering exceptional value and biblical encouragement to the masses.

ecpa Member of the
Evangelical Christian
Publishers Association

Printed in the United States of America.
05309 0216 BV

Dedication

To Andrew, Max, and Lincoln, who know the long road home and have enriched our lives immeasurably for taking it.

chapter 1

Captured!

Avery dragged her three-year-old brother behind a boxwood bush and listened for footsteps in the brittle leaves. She couldn't be sure which was louder—the person on their trail or her own heart, galloping like a stallion in her ears.

With one hand over Henry's mouth, Avery looked down at the nicest dress she owned. Not only had she torn the ruffles and destroyed the hem, but the white linen stood out in the shadowy woods, making her an easy target.

If she survived this afternoon and made it home tonight—and that felt like a giant *if*—her father would demand to know why her dress was stained with grass and mud and tinged with blood.

She would tell him the truth.

How could she possibly have known that a simple walk in the woods would turn dangerous? It was her thirteenth birthday, and she'd had no intention of spending the day cooped up in their small, dusty cottage, doing chores that would need to be done again tomorrow.

Now Avery was sure she heard twigs snap. Crows bolted, and she felt someone or something watching her. Her father would understand the ruined dress.

Clothes, after all, could be replaced.

People, as their family knew all too well, could not.

"Don't let go of my hand," Avery whispered as Henry wiggled. She squeezed his shoulder until he twisted his face and nodded.

He looked scared, and why wouldn't he? Instead of playing with the paper boat tucked in his pocket, he was hiding in the ghostly woods while a cold wind whistled through the trees.

"I'll figure a way to get us out of here," Avery whispered next to Henry's ear. "Just don't make a sound, and do exactly what I say."

Henry nodded, tears dotting the corners of his big brown eyes.

Normally, hiding behind a bush was a dumb idea. Tall and long legged, Avery was the fastest runner among her friends. No one laughed about her unusually big feet or made fun of her unruly inky hair, because she could outrun everyone, including the boys. She knew she could easily outpace someone in the woods—if she didn't have Henry.

So, while the unpleasant sounds of the woods rose up around them, Avery hatched a plan.

They would move to the one place she had always felt safe.

It was now or never.

Wait, the wind seemed to whisper, but Avery didn't obey.

Taking a deep breath and grabbing Henry's hand, she ducked from behind the boxwood. Head bent and body low, she pulled her brother to the next bush and the next until they reached a butternut tree deep in the thickets—but not just *any* butternut tree. This was where their father had built the most spectacular tree house when Avery was a little girl.

Rising before them stood a castle tree house—two stories high with an open turret and stairs that wound through a trap door that led to a tiny chamber at its highest point. The castle included a sky bridge, a tower prison, a tunnel, and a library—perfect for a girl with a bright imagination and a hunger for stories.

In the castle Avery could be anybody she wanted to be. On sunny days, she pretended to be queen and made Henry one of her loyal subjects. She painted watercolor castles and wrote poetry while sending Henry to collect blackberries or fetch water from the nearby stream for their snack. At night, when the sky was as black as ink, Avery would lie on the roof and imagine the stars were diamonds in her crown.

This castle held many secrets—among them, it supposedly sat atop an intricate system of tunnels—but whether any of them were true, Avery had no idea. Most importantly, it was the last place Avery saw her mother before she left and never came back.

Today it would be a hiding place.

Avery decided she and Henry would stay in the tree house until night fell, and then they would sneak home where Avery would explain everything to their father. He would be angry at first but would eventually soften. He might even loan her the money to buy a replacement dress since she had saved her brother's life.

Avery was just about to lead Henry into the arched doorway of the thick tree trunk when he yanked free of her grasp and raced into the open.

"Bronte!" he shouted, dropping to his knees and wrapping his pudgy arms around the mutt that was the family dog.

As Bronte's matted fur spattered Henry with mud, Avery's hopes of her father's forgiveness vanished.

She had been so sure she and Henry were in danger.

Dumb dog, she thought, both relieved and ashamed.

They were not being chased as she had suspected, but she had ruined her one good dress and Henry was covered in filth. Her father would say she had let her imagination get the best of her *again*, and she would spend the rest of her birthday alone in her bedroom, likely without any gifts or treats.

"Oh, Bronte," Avery said, joining Henry in scratching Bronte's floppy ears. She couldn't stay mad at the dog for long. They were the same age and had been best friends for as long as she could remember.

"Let's go home."

"But why?" Henry said, his voice rising to a whine the way it did when he was made to eat his vegetables or take a bath. "You said we were going to play hide-and-seek. Nobody found us."

"Good thing," Avery said. "But now it's time to go home for supper."

This news made Henry smile. "We'll have apple sausages and cheese," he said.

Avery was about to tell him they didn't know what their father had planned but that they would be grateful for whatever they were given. But then she heard it—

The snapping of twigs.

And she saw it—

The crows bolting.

And she felt it—

Someone or something was watching them.

And this time, Avery knew it wasn't the dog.

She grabbed Henry around the waist and ran as fast as she could move toward the tree house. But just as she leapt inside and shouted, "Hang on!" everything went dark.

All that remained was a bell clanging in the distance.

chapter 2

Trapped

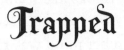

The cramped, dark cart smelled like boots left in the rain.

Avery sat with her back pressed against splintering boards, chin on her knees and her neck aching from leaning forward—for how long she had no idea, but the pain was intense. A salty, bitter rag covered her mouth, and she couldn't move her legs. Her stomach hurt more than it ever had, though she couldn't be sure if it was from hunger or something else.

Worse, she had no idea what had happened to Henry. The thought of him scared and hungry in another cart sent a fresh stab of pain through Avery's chest and she gasped for air.

I was supposed to protect him. I was the one who took him out of the house.

Suddenly, she realized the cart was moving.

She struggled to raise her hands—tied tightly at the wrists—and pounded the top of the cart as hard as she could manage until her knuckles stung.

Everything halted, and an old woman's bulging eyes appeared between the slats. Avery recoiled from hair that looked like long white wires and a face filled with so many creases she might easily be a hundred years old.

"So you're still alive!" the woman said, cackling. "Wasn't sure there for a while. I was wondering if I'd have to bury you out 'ere. Didn't want to mess with digging another grave." She smiled a gummy grin and added, "Looks like it might rain."

Another grave?

All Avery could see in her mind was Henry's scared face. She threw her body at the sides of the cart, hoping to break out, but the box wouldn't budge, and the woman stopped smiling.

"Relax," she said. "You're not going anywhere. This cart has been my sturdy companion longer than you've been on God's green earth."

Avery could see the woman wore a royal-blue cloak, and the tip of her nose was cherry red from the wind. Despite her age, her voice was strong and her black, beady eyes serious as a snake. "No banging and no yelling, you 'ear me? Or there will be consequences."

"I'm not scared of your threats," Avery said, her voice muffled by the rag around her mouth. "I'm stronger than you."

The woman smiled again, light dancing in her dull eyes. "But your brother's not. If you don't want anything to 'appen to 'enry, you'll be quiet."

He's still alive. This, at least, brought Avery a small measure of comfort.

The old woman began to laugh—a hollow, unhappy sound—revealing several missing teeth and a deep scar along her right cheek.

She knows Henry's name. What else does she know? How did she make him talk? What did he tell her?

Avery knew she should scream and hope someone would come. She could easily overpower the woman. How fast could an old woman run?

But she has Henry.

"Are you listening?" the woman said, slapping the cart with a hand as red as blood.

Avery nodded.

"You kids are all the same," the woman mumbled, wiping her forehead with the edge of her cloak. "So much trouble and so ungrateful." Her knuckles rose like mountains against the soft, flat flesh of her hand, and Avery saw a ruby ring that looked like it could be worth a fortune.

Who does she work for?

The old woman shuffled away, saying, "I almost forgot. 'appy birthday. Make a wish, darling."

The woman laughed again, the sound sending a rush of cold up Avery's spine. Then the woman disappeared and the cart began to bump along the road again.

Avery rested her chin back on her knees as hot tears sprang to her eyes. It was only supposed to be a walk. This was not how she had imagined spending her special day. She wished she could start the day over and do what her father instructed.

As her ruby flower necklace pressed against her collarbone, she knew she had made a terrible mistake to leave the house without her father's permission. He would look for them in the tree house, but he would have no idea where to look when he did not find them there.

A thick darkness settled, and with it, cold air.

Suddenly, the old woman began to sing in a voice as low as a man's—

> *Tonight the moon is watching as we ride toward the sea,*
> *The sky above, the ground below will sing in 'armony.*
> *"You're free!" we'll sing and "free!" again—You're free,*
> *young Avery.*

But Avery suspected her freedom had been left in her tree castle in the woods.

As the night grew colder, the woman slowed and her breathing grew loud and labored. The flat, gravel roads gave way to steep climbs and craggy hills, and Avery feared the old woman might have a heart attack and leave them both to freeze to death in the middle of nowhere.

Hours of travel felt like days.

Suddenly, Avery's sad and weary eyes settled on a scene that rose before the slats of the cart. Hundreds of brightly lit windows and dozens of turrets touched the sky, making the city in the distance look like a pyramid of gold perched on a pile of puffy clouds, a sort of glass castle illuminating the night sky. Its vibrant colors pulsed with life unlike anything Avery had ever seen. A thousand times she had imagined being found in a place that looked just like this—like it belonged in a fairy tale.

Her mother had spun tales of an evil king's castle—filled

with secret passageways and tunnels. Her stories about the underground colonies, which she called "the underworld," were the best. When she told them late at night by candlelight that cast wide shadows on the bare walls of their tiny house, Avery forgot everything else in the world, including the fact they were poor and hungry. Those moments, curled beside her mother in bed, were her most treasured memories.

Now her stomach twisted.

Every fairy tale has its dragon.

She longed for the apple sausages Henry had talked about in the woods. She would even settle for the thick pea pottage that made their usual meal. She didn't care about her ruined dress anymore, even if she owed her father a lifetime of Saturdays sweeping the endless dust from the floor of his shop to buy a new one. She just wanted to go home.

⁓∞⁓

Sloping rooftops and pointed turrets gave way to foreboding walls and dancing shadows so powerful they made Avery's heart sink. Whoever lived in this magnificent city on a hill had money and power, so this kidnapping wasn't about a ransom. Her father had nothing of value to offer rich people.

Eventually, the cart halted again and the woman barked an order to someone Avery couldn't see. Bartering ensued, followed by the clanking of coins, and the cart was pushed onto something that moved up and down slowly.

Avery pressed her face against the slats.

I'm being sold. To whom? For how much?

And then another thought was slow to follow—

Hopefully Henry and I are sold to the same person so we can stay together.

And then a final thought—

A raft. I don't know how to swim.

Chances of rescue looked slimmer by the second. Even if she escaped the box, she would never escape the water.

On the other side of the raft, another box bore another frightened face pressed against its slats. Their eyes met and held briefly before the boy—who looked to be about Avery's age—moved quickly out of Avery's view.

She turned her attention to the sea, where moonlight shimmered off choppy waves that made the raft bob, and she feared she might get sick.

I cannot make a scene if the risk is a watery grave.

The raft inched closer to the glowing city, its lights so dazzling that it looked as if it had been dusted with crystals. And it wasn't perched on puffy clouds after all, but on its own island.

The raft maneuvered around a thick tree trunk and glided smoothly over the glassy surface of the suddenly stilled water. The moon appeared large and lavender in its brilliance.

Avery knew that wherever she was going was unlike anywhere she had ever been.

For good or for evil—and she suspected evil—her life was about to change forever.

chapter 3

Kate

The raft came to a standstill, and the old woman pushed the cart onto dry land with a grunt.

She must have gotten a second wind during their ride on the raft, because she pushed with renewed energy over the winding hills to where a steep road led to a thick wooden door under an enormous towering archway. Two burly guards with pockmarked faces and chests as round as barrels stood on either side of the door, each holding a heavy torch in his hand with flames that licked the air and spit out heavy smoke as black as midnight.

One of the guards grunted and Avery felt the beat of her heart in her neck.

She was thankful, at least, to have survived the raft. Now she hoped to survive these men. She didn't have the energy to fight. And from the size of these two, she would need more than energy if they intended to harm her.

Avery suspected people did whatever these men required.

She could only hope that her father was out looking for her and Henry by now and that he had already alerted the authorities.

Of course he has. He is looking for us right now. We'll be home by breakfast.

"What's in the cart?" one of the guards asked, kicking the box with his enormous boot.

Avery moved as far back and out of sight as possible.

"Potatoes and blackberries," the old woman said, a surprising unease in her voice.

Avery didn't know whose side the men would take if she called for help, but she knew she had a better chance defending herself against the old woman than against men with muscles the size of bread bowls and boots the size of planets.

More words. More grunts. More kicking the cart.

Finally, they opened the door to a set of narrow limestone steps that seemed to lead forever up an unlit stairway. Before Avery had time to think about what it meant for her own cramped and aching back and legs—

Ka-thunk, ka-thunk, ka-thunk.

Someone—surely not the old woman—was dragging or pushing the cart up the steps one painful thud at a time. Avery slammed back against the boards, her head hitting the top and the sides and her knees knocking the front when she tried to brace herself. She wanted to cry out in agony, but who might hear her and what consequence might that bring? She bit down on the oily rag to keep from screaming. By the time the cart stopped, she ached all over and knew that even if she were able to escape, she wouldn't get far.

Was that the plan? *Injured birds never fly far.*

A door opened to a stream of welcoming, golden light, and all at once everything became pleasant. Avery longed for more of the warmth that came with the light, no matter the cost.

The cart creaked backward, stopped, and was pushed upright, and a crowd gathered around it.

Avery peered through the slats.

Shimmery fabric. Eager voices. Hushed tones. *Dirty feet.*

When the old woman spoke, the room fell silent.

"This one 'ere is feisty! She might bite." Nervous laughter rose like steam from broth. "You know the rules. Don't let 'er out of your sight even for a moment. If you can't break 'er will by morning, send for me, and I'll do it."

Avery didn't like the sound of that, but before she could think about it too long, the lid to the cart was lifted and Avery was dumped out, a tangled mess of dirty white dress and long, gnarly black hair.

The crowd gasped.

Avery lay on her back and groaned, staring at the heavily painted mosaic ceiling as the crowd closed in around her. A sea of dirty young faces swam into focus, easily fifty pairs of unblinking eyes taking her in. Dozens of well-dressed kids with hungry looks and wide, expectant gazes.

"What's her name?" a boy asked.

"Avery," the old woman answered, untying Avery's wrists and removing the cloth from her mouth.

Suddenly Avery sat up. "How do you know my name? What is this place, and why am I here? When can I go home? My father will find you and he'll prosecute you to the full extent of the law, I promise!"

"Like I said, feisty," the woman said, and she turned to leave.

Avery jumped to her feet and lunged, latching onto the woman's shoulders, intending to tackle her and pin her to the ground, but the woman shook her off with surprising effortlessness, fire burning in her black eyes. "Do not touch me, child!"

"Or what?" Avery shouted.

The woman swung a fist at Avery just as a pair of strong hands yanked Avery out of the way.

"I'll handle her," a deep voice said.

"Then teach 'er to show some respect. I should have left 'er in the woods to rot."

"Rotting might have been the better option!" Avery bit back.

Snickers went up from the crowd.

The woman disappeared into a dark stairwell and slammed the door as Avery turned to see who had spared her from the punch.

The boy was tall, with shaggy brown hair and alarming green eyes bright as sea glass.

"You're welcome," he offered with a smile.

"Next time, don't interfere!" Avery said louder than she intended.

He raised his hands. "Okay." Then, leaning closer, he added, "But at least talk to Kate. She's nice. She'll help you."

"Who's Kate?" Avery snapped.

He pointed to a girl with strawberry-blond hair, warm brown eyes, and delicate cheekbones. She stood out from the crowd because of her clean face and blue-blooded posture.

And slippers.

Kate stepped forward and put a hand on Avery's arm.

"Come with me," she said quietly.

And against her better judgment, Avery followed. But as they approached a dark hallway with no end in sight, she had a feeling that the worst of the day was yet to come.

chapter 4

The News

Arm in arm, Kate led Avery in silence down a long, narrow hallway lit by flickering candles on tall stands. A chill rose up around them as they walked.

Finally, in a wood-paneled room with a long, rough-hewn table and dozens of straight, wooden chairs, Avery eased away from Kate and moved to stand on the other side of the table to put space between them.

Trust no one.

Avery didn't want this refined girl being too nice to her. They weren't going to be friends. As soon as she found Henry, they would race for home. She would carry him all night if she needed to. She would even let him talk endlessly about what they would eat for breakfast. She didn't even care if her father forbade her from leaving the house for the rest of her life or yelled at her until morning.

"Do you have any idea why you're here?" Kate asked in a small voice.

"How could I? I don't even know where I am."

"Don't be mad. Everyone is mad on arrival, but there's no point. You'll figure out soon that we all want the same things."

"What do you know about what I want?"

Kate paused and seemed to look kindly at Avery for a long time. "Freedom."

Avery couldn't argue with that.

Kate continued, "Be patient. Answers will come in time."

"I don't have time. I need answers now. Where are we, and why am I here?"

"It's complicated, but I promise you that following the rules will give you your best chance of survival."

"What kind of rules?"

"No outside contact is allowed for any reason. And you must stay quiet."

Avery was too tired to think and too tired to argue with someone she didn't even know. She had no desire to play games with this girl. Why had the boy with the shaggy hair promised that she would be helpful? So far she was as useful as a red-bellied turtle.

Avery pressed her fingers to her temples.

"You'd better sit," Kate said softly. "There's more."

Avery didn't want to do anything this girl suggested, but because she was exhausted and sore, she collapsed into a chair as Kate moved to sit across from her, a gigantic bowl of fruit between them.

Kate's perfect hair, the string of glass beads at her neck, and her gold-colored dress that shimmered in the candlelight made Avery wonder what she must look like in comparison.

Not good.

"I have one important question," Kate said. "Are you thirteen?"

Avery had almost forgotten it was her birthday. She nodded miserably.

"Interesting," Kate said as a sort of relief seemed to wash over her.

"Why does it matter?"

"Everyone here is thirteen," Kate continued. "You were the second person brought here today."

The boy from the raft. "Where is he?"

"Sleeping."

Avery snorted and shook her head. She couldn't imagine letting herself relax enough to fall asleep in this place.

Suddenly ravenous, she pulled an orange from the bowl, peeled it, and began to eat, the juice running down her arm. And it was the strangest thing. The fruit was the best thing Avery had ever tasted. Unable to stop herself, she ate the pulp, the juice, and even the peel.

As Avery licked the stickiness off her arm, Kate smiled. "I'm on your side. I'm not your enemy."

"I don't care. I'm not staying long enough to make enemies. Henry and I need to be free of here tonight."

Kate nodded. "Everyone who arrives says the same thing."

Suddenly, Avery remembered she hadn't seen her brother since arriving—

"Where is Henry?"

Kate averted her eyes.

"Where is he?"

At Kate's solemn stare, Avery pounded the table.

"I don't know," Kate blurted. "I didn't want to tell you, but we're all separated from our brothers and sisters. But doing what we're told keeps them alive."

Keeps them alive? Avery couldn't speak. *Oh, sweet Henry!*

Tears clouded her vision and the room began to spin. She had assumed Henry was traveling in a box behind her all along and was now being entertained by a group of girls in another room. When Kate said, "Everyone here is thirteen," she meant it.

Henry isn't here. He is lost. And it's my fault.

She suddenly wanted nothing more than to feel his sticky hand in hers and to hear his endless chatter.

And she knew with sudden certainty she would kill anyone who hurt him, starting with the old woman.

Kate placed a hand on Avery's arm, but Avery shoved it away and feared she would be sick. She stifled a scream that rose from the pit of her stomach and whispered, "Help me," as thousands of pinpricks filled her head and her breathing grew labored.

Kate called for someone, and soon Avery heard a voice that seemed far away but sounded like the boy with the shaggy hair.

"You're going to be okay," he said. "I will help you." Then to Kate, "Does she know where we are yet? Did you tell her?"

"She's not ready to know the truth."

chapter 5

Choosing Colors

When Avery came to her senses, she was in a large, musty room filled with dozens of lumpy mattresses lined side by side and topped with drab, woolen blankets. A few wooden wardrobes lined the plain walls, and a gray stone fireplace cast a weak glow.

She slid her gaze to Kate, who sat unmoving on the floor beside her.

Avery pushed herself up, her head throbbing. "How long did I sleep?"

"Maybe an hour. Are you hungry? Everyone else is finished eating, and if you miss a meal, you're usually out of luck, but I know where the supplies are kept."

"I'm fine."

It was a lie. Avery's stomach churned with hunger, but she couldn't imagine keeping anything down.

"This is where you will sleep tonight," Kate continued. "The girls occupy this room and another just like it, and the boys live in two down the hall."

Kate held out her hand and uncurled her fingers to reveal Avery's ruby flower necklace. Glancing both ways, she said quietly, "Keep this close to you. Things go missing here every day.

I'd hate for this to disappear."

Avery lunged for it, yanking it out of Kate's hand and putting it back around her neck. Why Kate had taken it off in the first place Avery had no idea. This necklace was her only link to home and everything she held dear.

"One more thing," Kate said, nodding toward the heavy velvet drapes that covered the windows, making the room darker than necessary. "We're not allowed to look outside."

"Says who?"

"*They* are always watching," Kate said, barely above a whisper. "They know when we break rules or when we try to escape. Terrible things happen, Avery. For Henry's sake, you must believe me."

Avery wanted to ask more, but a shriek from the doorway prevented further discussion. Avery looked over to see a group of girls marching toward her, beautifully dressed, but with dirty faces and unkempt hair. The contrast between their fancy clothes and muddy skin confused her. One girl had enough dirt caked under her fingernails to plant a garden.

Their arms swung in unison, and they wore black ribbons on their right wrists.

"You're in my bed," the leader said. She had straight, wheat-colored hair and a nose that turned up slightly. She also had the longest eyelashes Avery had ever seen, but they did nothing to improve her dull eyes.

"I'm sorry. I didn't know. I passed out and—"

"Now you do. So go."

"Come on, Ilsa," Kate said. "She needed a place to—"

"Well, she can't use my bed. She smells like a horse."

One of Ilsa's friends laughed, which only seemed to encourage Ilsa.

"Look at her awful dress. For all I know, she has fleas."

"She's had a bad day," Kate said. "Just let her go."

"It would be a bad day for me, too, if I were forced to wear that silly necklace." She reached out and flicked the ruby flower so that it swung behind Avery's shoulder.

Again, Ilsa's friend chortled behind her.

Avery felt something hot grow inside. This necklace was the last gift she had ever received from her mom, so it meant more than she could possibly explain to a stranger. Her mother had placed it around her neck and told her to wear it every day, and even though it was large and heavy, Avery had obeyed. To her, it was the most beautiful piece of jewelry in the world, even if it was a little gaudy.

She rose and came face-to-face with Ilsa.

"What is wrong with you? You don't even know me."

"I know more than you think I do," Ilsa said. "I saw you acting like a lunatic out there. Stay away from me and stay away from Tuck."

"Tuck?"

"Don't pretend you don't know him. Twice in one night you needed his help. Really? You're a good actress, Avery, but just so you know, he'll help anyone. Don't flatter yourself."

The boy with the shaggy hair. This whole conversation is because of a boy?

"Don't worry; I didn't read into anything," Avery promised.

"Keep it that way."

"Let's go, Avery," Kate said.

But when Ilsa glanced down at the flower necklace and smirked, Avery shoved her with all her might, sending her flying back onto a nearby mattress.

Ilsa staggered to her feet and sauntered back, standing nose to nose with Avery. "You've just started something you won't be able to finish. Watch your back," Ilsa said, before heading toward the door with her flock of ladies in tow. "And don't let that necklace out of your sight!"

"I'm not scared of you," Avery called after her, but it sounded weak.

Kate smiled politely. "It would probably be a good idea for you to sleep in the other bunk room. Come with me."

❦

Avery sat on her new bed waiting for Kate to scold her for what she had done.

"You picked the right bed," Kate said finally. "Right next to mine."

"Why did those girls wear black ribbons on their wrists?"

Kate rolled her eyes. "It's a silly little game they've created to occupy their time here. Once a group forms, they wear matching colors. If there's a falling out, a girl can leave and wear a ribbon of a different color."

Avery looked at Kate's bare wrist.

"I try to be everyone's friend," Kate said.

"Then shouldn't you be wearing everyone's ribbon?"

Kate laughed until she fell back onto her mattress. Soon—despite her fear and dread—Avery was laughing, too. It had been the second most horrible day of her life, but she was laughing with a girl she had just met in a place she had never been.

When the laughter subsided, Kate said, "Believe it or not, you'll see that it's not too bad here, even if we *are* here against our will and there *are* guards at all the exit doors."

"Then why won't you tell me where we are?"

"I will, but you need to get your strength back first."

✺

Avery was relieved when Kate showed her the copper tub and the soap made of olive oil. Never in her life had a bath felt so good. She soaked her weary muscles, scrubbed the mud off her legs and arms, and washed her hair before returning to the bunk room, leaving a trail of watery footprints as she went.

As she wound through the rows of beds to find her own, she noticed dozens of girls were in theirs, whispering and giggling. It didn't seem to Avery like they were as concerned about being kidnapped as she felt. This made no sense.

She was grateful to find a clean, white nightgown—floor-length with long sleeves—laid out on her bed. She had feared she would be stuck in her dirty white dress until she returned home. She changed quickly, the fabric softer than any she had ever felt, and slipped under the blankets.

She sank into the mattress, a welcome relief to her sore body, and waited until the candles were extinguished and the room settled under a haze of smoke. In the dark, she quietly ripped the seam at one end of her pillow and slipped off the ruby flower necklace. She tucked it into the feathers of the pillow, determined to keep it safe until she was able to head back home.

Losing that necklace would be like losing her mother all over again.

She couldn't handle losing anything else.

Avery glanced around the room to make sure no one saw.

Only Kate stared back, unblinking.

Avery lay on her back, eyes adjusting to the dark, staring at the intricate detail on a ceiling that belonged in a cathedral, not in a musty room where kids were being held against their will. Her eyes suddenly felt heavy, and sleep called to her.

"If you stay," Kate whispered, so faintly Avery could barely hear her, "I'll find a way to give you back your brother and your mother."

You're dreaming. You haven't even told Kate about your mother.

But Kate's wry smile was the last thing Avery saw before she surrendered to sleep.

chapter 6

Food Fight

Starving, Avery awoke to smells she had never experienced.

She stood for a long moment staring at her clothes, laid out for her at the end of her bed. Mysteriously, her tattered white dress had been replaced by a beautiful gown unlike anything she had ever worn at home.

Home. Already the word felt so foreign.

The dress was made of the softest green satin, the neckline trimmed with a thousand tiny stars that gleamed in the candlelight and reminded her of the ones she admired from her castle tree house rooftop in the woods.

She wriggled out of her nightgown and tugged the dress over her shoulders. Her hair needed brushing, and she found a comb and a heavy, gold-gilded hand mirror on a nearby mattress, so out of place in the plain, dark room.

When she held it before her, a fresh mark on her left wrist made her drop the mirror onto the mattress and forget about her hair.

She ran her fingers over the raised black star, the size of a copper coin. It didn't hurt, thank goodness, but neither could she rub it off.

Who put this here and when? How did I sleep through it?

Avery found that her muddy black boots had been replaced by beautiful red slippers with tiny, shiny beads, and someone had correctly guessed her unusually large shoe size.

The only other girl who wore slippers was Kate.

Everything about this place led to more questions than answers.

After breakfast, her first order of business would be to find out exactly where she was and who was holding her against her will.

After breakfast, she thought, as another wave of delicious smells hit her.

Avery retrieved her necklace from her pillow and slid it over her head, tucking the flower beneath the fabric of her dress, and followed the scent of the food.

⚜

Avery had never seen so many well-dressed kids in one place. Some stood in clusters talking excitedly. A dozen carried platters of fruit and meat, breads dripping with icing, and thick, silver mugs filled to the brim with milk.

This was not what Avery was accustomed to eating. At home, meals consisted of what she or her father caught while fishing, hunting, or trapping or what they had grown in their garden.

Kate appeared at her side with a chirpy, "Good morning," and tugged her toward the table. "I saved you a seat." She filled Avery's plate with all kinds of wonderful things, saying, "We eat like this at every meal, so pace yourself."

That's when Avery saw the black star on Kate's left wrist— matching her own.

"We all have one," Kate mumbled.

"Why?"

"If you escape, the mark will identify you and they'll bring you back." Kate looked around before adding quietly, "Or they'll send you to the Forbidden City."

Avery had so many questions, but they would have to wait until she and Kate were alone.

Nothing is certain and no one is safe.

Meanwhile, she ate. Sweet gave way to salty, and cold gave way to warm. The grapes alone were bigger and better than any she had ever tasted. She had no idea how she would describe all this to Henry. He would ask her to retell the story a dozen times.

Her father would say she was exaggerating again, but she would deny it.

When a steaming mug of coffee was placed in front of her, Avery thought she might cry. Her father had always mixed a tiny bit with milk for her and Henry when business was good. This coffee was pure and undiluted, and she drank it like water, feeling renewed energy surge within her.

As she was finishing the last of what tasted like bread with cinnamon and a hint of orange, Avery spotted Ilsa at the center of the table and returned the unfinished bite to her plate, her appetite gone.

Ilsa stared at her smugly. "I'm watching you," she mouthed.

Avery shrugged.

Next to Ilsa sat a boy who looked like her twin, with wheat-colored hair and a turned-up nose. Avery wondered if he was as hostile as his sister.

On Ilsa's other side sat Tuck, his shaggy hair swept to one side this morning.

"Tuck is a good person," Kate said quietly, and Avery realized she was staring.

"I don't care. Any friend of Ilsa's is no friend of mine."

But suddenly she had a strong urge to get to know Tuck, if only to frustrate Ilsa. He looked happy and confident, talking kindly to everyone around him. Avery suspected he made everyone he spoke to feel important. She also thought he looked older than thirteen. He was tall, broad shouldered, and assertive. Suddenly, he locked eyes with her, and she found it impossible to look away. He lifted an eyebrow, and she felt her face flush.

What is wrong with me? I've never cared about boys, and I don't need to start now.

From the far end of the table, shouts erupted and a pair of boys began throwing punches. Friends joined in, and handfuls of meat and fruit flew as insults were traded and chairs were knocked backward.

Tuck jumped to his feet and began peeling bodies off each other.

"What's going on?" Avery asked Kate, who seemed unfazed.

"It happens almost every morning." And then just as casually she said, "Would you like to look around? I could give you a tour that would answer many of your questions."

Would I ever.

"Let's go."

chapter 7

The Stairwell

Avery hugged her arms tight against her body, the thin material of her dress doing little to keep her warm as she and Kate stood at the top of a long flight of eerily dark limestone steps.

These are the steps I was carted up yesterday.

Avery could see the door at the bottom, only this morning a heavy chain hung across its center and a thick lock hung from the latch.

"Promise you'll do what I say," Kate said, the smile gone from her eyes. "What we're about to do could get us in a lot of trouble if we're caught. I need to trust you to do exactly as I tell you and not speak until I say you can."

Avery nodded, but when a fat rat scurried over her slipper, she kicked and yelped until Kate clamped a hand over her mouth. "Rule number one: quiet in the stairwell!"

Only when Avery nodded again did Kate release her hand.

They took the stairs quickly, passing several girls moving up and down, their dresses whooshing as they went.

Kate whispered, "This one stairwell winds around the building's four hundred forty rooms, designed so that the staff can work without being seen. There are eighty-four flights of stairs."

Avery's eyes widened. Was it possible the city she had seen from the raft was only one large building? But who could afford such a place?

They continued descending the stairs. At each landing they passed a thick wooden door with black metal latches. Some doors were painted with a giant red *X*; others were not.

"What's inside?" Avery asked after they had passed half a dozen.

"Each door leads to another room. Rule number two: never open a door with an *X* on it."

"Why?"

"Just don't."

Avery opened her mouth to ask something else, but the look on Kate's face stopped her.

Finally, they paused on a landing where Kate pressed her ear against a door then grabbed Avery's arm and led her inside to a pastry wonderland with shelves of tiny cakes and pots of candied peanuts. Loaves of bread baked in corner brick ovens emitting wisps of smoke in delicate curls.

A group of girls around a large table rolled dough and argued playfully about something Avery couldn't decipher.

"Everything you will eat is made in here," Kate said.

When Avery didn't respond, Kate clutched her arm. "This is important." She pointed to a brass bell in the corner of the ceiling. "There's one of those in the corner of every room. Boys called scouts alert us when an adult comes anywhere near any of the rooms where we spend our time. When we hear the bell, we go directly to the stairwell, no matter what we're doing. Nothing is as important as staying hidden from the adults in this building. Do you understand?"

Avery nodded. But, of course, she didn't understand.

"You are never more than ten feet from a scout."

Avery wondered how many people could see her at any given moment. She twirled slowly, waving nervously in case a scout was watching.

In case Tuck is watching. . . Is he a scout?

Why was she complicating things by thinking about a boy?

And why were they hiding from adults?

Kate led her through the kitchen into a dark room full of long wooden shelves loaded with canned goods, wedges of cheese, and bags of flour and sugar. Kate tore open a bag and handed Avery two brown pieces of something that smelled good.

"Try it," she said.

Avery snapped off a bite. She liked the way it sent a zing of flavor through her mouth.

"It's called chocolate," Kate said, smiling.

Avery would have asked for more if she hadn't just eaten enough breakfast to feed her entire village back home. She wished she had pockets so she could hide a piece for Henry.

Kate pointed to the floor. "Circulation vents," she whispered. "They allow air to travel throughout the building. The scouts use them to track the adults. It's why I brought you here."

Again, Avery wanted to ask why they were hiding from the adults, but Kate pressed a finger to her lips and motioned for

Avery to join her as she knelt by the metal grate on the floor and quietly cranked open the slats with a heavy handle.

Avery peered through the vent.

A man with thick silver hair sat at a desk, his head in his hands. Avery felt like a bird looking down at a statue. She thought for a moment how fun it would be to drop a piece of chocolate on his head, and this made her giggle.

Kate glared at her.

The man seemed somehow large and small at the same time, hunched over piles of papers and open books.

A door burst open near the man's desk, and a woman entered and began pacing in front of him. She was small with snow-white skin and fire-red ringlets piled on her head in the shape of an elaborate bees' nest. Her hairdo was so big it made the rest of her body look unnaturally small.

Avery stifled a laugh.

Again, Kate narrowed her eyes.

The woman wore a midnight-blue dress with a cinched waist and a high collar. Its train whipped behind her as she paced, while heavy strands of pearls dripped from her neck and wrists.

She acts like she owns the place. Maybe she does.

Avery guessed the woman to be in her twenties, younger than the man but every bit as powerful, maybe more. Avery put her ear against the vent.

"What more do you want from me, Angelina? I've done everything you've asked, given you everything you've ever wanted."

"Are you kidding?" the woman snapped, her voice climbing to a whine. "You keep promising we will be married, but how long do you want me to wait? How long do you expect me to keep your secrets?"

The man started coughing—loud, sputtering, watery coughs that made Avery want to take him a cup of water or at least clear her own throat.

The talking stopped, and Avery pulled her ear away and looked to make sure she wasn't missing anything. At that moment, the man looked up as if searching for the right words, and Avery froze.

Could he see her? She moved away just in case, but as she did, she realized she recognized his face.

chapter 8

Figuring It Out

Avery scrupulously ran the man's features through the catalog of her memory.

Matching his thick silver hair was a short-cropped beard, tough olive skin, and bushy eyebrows. His cheekbones protruded, and deep wrinkles crisscrossed his face.

He was definitely much older than the woman he called Angelina, but younger than the old woman from the woods.

He is definitely important.

Avery had no memory of the red-haired woman, but even before the man cut Angelina off with an impatient wave, Avery knew he was wearing a large gold ring with a ruby stone. She had seen it in her mind's eye even before he waved his hand and confirmed it.

Where have I seen him before?

He was saying something sternly about wanting to get married but not having time to plan a ceremony because of official business abroad due to shifting alliances.

Shifting alliances?

"Your lectures bore me," Angelina said in a childish voice, sitting on the corner of his desk and dangling her legs over the side.

"I have a country!" he roared, but Avery wasn't paying attention. She was plundering her past for the remnants of any story that would make this scenario make sense. At least two—maybe three—decades separated the man and woman in the room, and they didn't appear to love each other. Yet they were discussing marriage.

And what does all of this have to do with my capture and imprisonment?

Kate had specifically said this tour would answer many of her questions.

Frustration gnawed at her.

Angelina was now pacing the marble floor, her heels clacking as she went. The familiar man was now standing.

Angelina turned and plunged a finger into his chest.

"If you think I've forgotten everything you said, you are even crazier than your people say you are. No one is as good for you as I am. Marry me and make it permanent in the next month."

"Or what?"

"Or I will kill. . . All. Of. Them. And I will make sure everyone knows it is your fault."

She added a trill of laughter as pinpricks traveled up Avery's spine. This woman seemed capable of whatever she promised.

The man appeared about to respond when the slats clapped shut and Kate, agitated, stood and walked away. Avery trailed her to the stairwell, and as soon as the door closed behind them, she grabbed Kate's arm. "It was just getting good! Why did you do that?"

"You've seen too much already."

"But you're wrong. I haven't seen *enough*."

"You promised to obey my rules on this tour. It's time to go." Kate turned to take the stairs.

"I know who he is," Avery blurted.

Kate stopped but did not turn around. "Okay, who is he?"

Avery bit her lip, still uncertain, but it was there on the edge of her memory.

Back in their bunk room, Kate said something about needing to get some work done and disappeared before Avery could follow. Just as well. Avery was tired, and Kate looked flustered after Angelina threatened to kill people. Why it mattered to Kate, Avery had no idea, unless Angelina was referring to killing *them*.

Avery flopped onto her mattress and stared at the ceiling, wondering what had happened. Kate didn't seem the fearful type, though she did seem to be holding back a lot of information.

Avery traced the elaborate arches, caught up in the intricate detail of the slopes and trellises until sleep began calling her name.

Her body bruised from travel and her mind overloaded from mystery, her breathing slowed and her eyelids grew heavy. She was just about to surrender to sleep when something came to her so clearly it was like a slap in the face, and she sat up.

She had been with her mother at a museum in the theater district when they stopped to admire a portrait that stretched the entire length of a wall. The painting featured a handsome man— dark haired and richly dressed—wearing a ruby ring. When Avery turned to ask her mother about the man's identity, she saw that her mom was crying.

"Mom?"

Avery's mother had brushed away her tears impatiently. *"You'll understand someday,"* she said. And then she had taken the ruby necklace she was wearing and placed it around Avery's neck with one instruction: *"Wear this every day. Never lose it. Do you understand?"*

Avery nodded.

And now she knew with certainty.

The man she had seen through the grate was the man from the portrait in the museum.

She now understood this with confidence.

Suddenly, she heard her mother's voice in her head—years of stories unwinding in slow motion. She thought her mother had only been inventing the stories as a distraction from the hunger they always felt. Now she knew better. She only needed to verify it.

She ran from the bunk room down the hall and into the stairwell, taking the stairs two at a time until she came to the door of her choice.

No red X.

She pressed her ear against it as she had seen Kate do and she flung it open.

The room on the other side of the door was exactly as she thought it would be.

As quickly as she had opened the door, she closed it and climbed more stairs. Again she pressed her ear to a door, pushed it open, and found what she expected.

She did this several times until her suspicions were proven correct.

And when she was sure of herself, she went in search of Kate.

❦

Kate sat in a tight circle of thirteen-year-olds—which included Tuck—talking quietly near a crackling fire in a stone hearth. When Avery approached, they fell silent and looked uncomfortable.

"I know where we are," Avery said, her heart hammering. She did not miss the look that passed between them.

Kate said softly, "We're listening."

"There's a turret and stairs that wind through a trapdoor and stop in a secret chamber at the highest point," Avery said in a rush. "I found the sky bridge, so I assume there is a tower prison, a tunnel, and a library. I haven't found them yet, but I will."

The kids sat like statues.

"We are prisoners in an evil king's castle."

chapter 9

The Announcement

Avery expected laughter or sarcastic replies.

But the group just stared at her.

"I grew up hearing about this place," she continued. "Songs and stories I thought my mother had made up to entertain me. Now that I think about it, I don't know why my mother knew so much about this castle, but she did. She described the rooms perfectly."

Still nothing.

"I can tell you anything you want to know. Except how long we'll be stuck here and any details about the redhead." Her voice cracked on the last word.

Was that a giggle?

Avery turned to leave, embarrassed she had even tried. She was starting to believe she didn't belong anywhere in the world.

"You're right," Tuck said, standing. "We are prisoners in the king's castle."

"We are?" Avery asked, unsure whether to be pleased or scared she was right.

He motioned her closer. "Sit with us and tell us everything you know. Maybe you can offer something that will help."

The group seemed to exhale at Tuck's willingness to include her. Kate patted the seat beside her.

"You've known all along?" Avery whispered as she sat.

Kate nodded. "To be in our inner circle, we need to know we can trust you. If Tuck trusts you, everyone else will, too."

"Does everyone else know?"

"That we're in the king's castle?" Kate nodded. "Eventually they all figure it out, though not usually as quickly as you."

Avery rehearsed her mother's stories for the group, every detail she could remember. It was nice talking about her mother again, if only for information. "So why are we here?"

A girl burst out laughing and was shushed.

A boy said, "You don't get out much, do you?"

Avery felt the red creep into her cheeks again.

Getting out was what got her in this mess to begin with.

Tuck took over explaining. "A month ago, the castle ordered that all thirteen-year-olds without living parents were to be"—he paused—"discarded."

The group seemed to tense at the word. Tuck continued.

"Entire bands of men have been sent to find and capture as many thirteen-year-old orphans as possible. If you step one foot outside of this castle, the star on your wrist will identify you and you will be destroyed."

Avery looked at Kate, who said simply, "The old woman brought us here to hide in the one place she's sure the king will never look—right under his nose in his own castle. And she's hidden our brothers and sisters somewhere else so that we won't leave. If we leave, we will never see them again."

Avery ignored this last bit. She couldn't imagine never seeing Henry again.

"What's in it for her?" Avery asked.

"Help," Kate said. "The castle is severely understaffed by a crippling workload because Angelina doesn't trust anyone. We live in the rooms once filled with the people who ran this castle."

"So we work in exchange for safety," Avery said.

Kate nodded. "The old woman passes along responsibilities and we do them. Anything a working adult can do in a castle, we can do."

"So then why do we avoid all adults?" Avery asked.

"Because we don't know which ones we can trust. Each of us has a large bounty on our head—any of the staff left in this castle could retire on the money made from turning us all in to the king."

Avery nodded. This, at least, made sense.

Tuck continued, "Every kid here is a thirteen-year-old orphan."

"Not me," Avery said.

This drew strange looks and murmurs. "Your parents are alive?" a boy asked.

"My father was working at his shop when I was taken from the woods."

"And your mother?"

A lump rose in Avery's throat. Who would believe her mom vanished almost two years ago but was never declared dead? Avery just shook her head.

"You're sure your father is still alive?" Tuck asked.

Avery nodded. "Of course! And he's probably very unhappy with me at the moment."

"If that's true, you're the only one here who isn't an orphan."

Avery could tell the group was not convinced. She had a strong urge to prove them wrong. She would find a way.

⁓❈⁓

By suppertime, a stack of news bulletins had made its way to the kids' quarters bearing the headline THE KING CHOOSES A QUEEN.

Avery and Kate huddled over the bulletin in a small sitting room off the dining room.

Other clusters of girls did the same.

"I don't understand. What is so special about Angelina?" Avery asked.

Kate glanced both ways before whispering, "Right now the king's family is in jeopardy of dying out. Without a son, the family name is doomed. Angelina is young and beautiful and has promised him an heir."

"But can't he marry anyone he chooses? Why not at least pick someone who is nice?"

"Angelina knows too many secrets. She has made the king dependent on her guidance and now she has given him no choice. He either marries her or risks her telling the world everything she knows."

"I have a feeling this isn't going to end well for anyone, including us."

"I don't know," Kate said. "Maybe a royal wedding is what this castle needs."

"You saw the way they fought in his office! They don't love each other."

"Marriages of power are rarely made of love."

⊶∞⊷

Avery missed Henry more than she thought possible.

She missed his silly questions and stubborn opinions, his pink cheeks and endless talk of food. She wished she had told him she loved him that last afternoon in the woods. She knew he must be terrified wherever he was, and that thought haunted her most of all.

She vowed not to leave the castle unless she was sure doing so wouldn't put Henry in more danger. There was simply no other choice. She was beginning to wonder if Henry and the other brothers and sisters were being held somewhere else in the castle. It was certainly big enough for everyone.

She would risk her life, if necessary, to find him.

⊶∞⊷

Avery spent her second and third mornings in the castle trying to make pies with the girls in the kitchen.

She almost set the place on fire.

With the room full of smoke, she said, "I didn't really pay attention when my mom tried to teach me to bake."

"We can tell," one said, who, like the others, looked shaken. No one protested when Avery said she thought she should find another job.

Ilsa and her friends worked in the laundry, so that was out. Pot wash sounded like eternal punishment, and the infirmary—for sick kids—was fully staffed, or so they said.

Avery had neither the skill nor the desire to join the woodworking team or the horticulture group. And the scouts laughed when she inquired there.

"Because I'm a girl?" she asked.

"Because you talk too much!"

Avery couldn't argue.

If only the castle needed an organist or an artist.

She went looking for Kate by climbing the stairs and stopping outside one of the topmost rooms where at least a dozen girls spent their days creating patterns, cutting fabrics, and sewing clothes. When she peeked in and saw what was featured on the mannequin, her hand flew to her mouth.

She had never seen anything like it.

chapter 10

The Crown

In the center of the sewing room stood a dazzling wedding dress. Yards of ivory silk gave way to lace and tiny pearls that shimmered in the light of a dozen candle stands.

Girls scurried around it as if dancing, their feet barely touching the floor, making small stitches and adding tiny pearls and diamonds as they went. A few hummed in harmony as they worked; others whispered and laughed.

Avery was drawn to the group like a moth to light, desperate to be included in the fun.

How—kept against their will—could these girls be so happy?

All Avery could think about was finding Henry and going home.

Kate came to stand beside her and answered without being asked. "They didn't have anything before coming here. Two of the girls you're looking at lived in a sewer. Now they have warm beds at night and full plates of food at every meal. They spend their days doing what they love with people they like. For most of them, this life in the castle is more than they ever had at home."

Avery took one step closer to the dress and the seamstresses set down their tools and shuffled out of the room.

Avery shot Kate a puzzled glance.

"Their work is done for the day," she said simply.

Avery was thankful for a few minutes with the dress all to herself. It was an image she wanted to burn in her memory forever.

Time seemed to stand still as she approached it, and a heavy spotlight appeared, leaving everything else in darkness, highlighting the gown's absolute perfection. She touched the delicate rope of pearls sewn at the waist, imagining what it would be like to wear such a dress in the presence of an entire kingdom.

"I've never seen anything more beautiful, Kate," she whispered. "Have you?"

"A dress is only as beautiful as the woman in it."

Avery wondered why everything Kate said sounded like a cryptic proverb. She sounded so much older than thirteen. Had Kate had a wise mother, too?

"How did you make this dress so fast?"

"A lot of us work here," Kate said.

"But a dress like this had to take hundreds of hours, and Angelina's been engaged for one day. It's nearly finished!"

Kate let out a sigh. "You ask a lot of questions."

"And you avoid straight answers."

They held each other's gaze in a friendly standoff.

Kate finally lowered her eyes. "Fine. We knew it was only a matter of time. And Angelina has very specific expectations. We knew if we waited until the dress was commissioned, we wouldn't have enough time to get it done. We can't have her sniffing around here because she might find out a group of kids made her dress, so we've been working on it for a while."

"You knew the engagement was coming before the king did?"

Kate nodded.

"And you don't find that strange?"

Kate glanced at the door then leaned close. "I've been trying to tell you. This place is full of secrets—centuries of them. The less you ask, the better. You don't want to be held accountable for what you know." Then, more brightly, she added, "Come. I want to show you something."

⸎

Avery followed Kate to where a full-length mirror was propped against the wall next to a heavily draped window. Kate pulled from behind it a red silk pillow bearing a queen's crown, and suddenly Avery could not speak.

She was not often at a loss for words, but this crown hushed her.

How many nights—curled in bed beside her mother while rain beat against the windows—had she described exactly this piece?

The crown was set in gold with dozens of elaborate gold stems topped with diamonds that caught the candlelight and danced in their opulence. Avery thought it looked like a cake topped with candles, but why anyone would ever put candles on a cake, she had no idea. This was the stuff of dreams—the crown every girl imagined when playing princess on summer days. Avery herself had pretended to wear a crown exactly like this when she played in her castle tree house in the woods. How many times had she closed her eyes and imagined the weight of it on her head?

"This will become Angelina's on her wedding day," Kate said.

"How are you even allowed to touch it?"

Kate laughed. "It's my job. Go ahead, try it on."

Avery shook her head, knowing better than to think the daughter of a peasant had any business trying on the crown of a queen. But before she could refuse, Kate placed it on her head.

Avery nearly fainted.

She stepped before the mirror and remembered what her mother had always told her. "Avery, girl, you can be anything God wants you to be. Even the queen if that is His plan."

She had always known her mother was just trying to encourage her the way mothers do. She hadn't actually believed the words.

"It's heavy," Avery said.

Kate nodded. "As are the pressures that come with the crown. Angelina will spend the rest of her life fearing the assassin's blade or the enemy's cup."

But Avery didn't hear any of this. Instead, she turned this way and that, admiring her look from every angle. It was impossible, she decided, to look bad in a crown like this.

❦

Kate and Avery sat and talked all afternoon, tucked away where they wouldn't be heard. When they finally stood to go downstairs for supper, Kate said, "Don't leave the castle until it's your only choice, okay? Being here may be what you were born to do."

Avery nodded, but as she did, she felt bad for making a promise she could not keep. She wouldn't stay one moment longer than she needed to. She only stayed now with the hope that she might find Henry or at least keep him safe.

She trusted that she would find her brother or that her father would find her before a week had passed. This hope kept her from doing anything too irrational.

The inner voice that so often got Avery into trouble whispered to her now. It told her to disappear from supper with a match.

As usual, she was prepared to do something she might regret.

chapter 11

Midnight Foray

Avery waited until everyone in the bunk room fell asleep.

The last thing the children did each night before bed was blow out the candles throughout their side of the castle, the trails of smoke long and thin and wobbly as the warm scent of day's end followed them all to bed.

It was eerily quiet now.

Barefoot in her white nightgown, she crossed the cold marble floor, resolve growing with each step to find the answer to a question that had gnawed at her since she'd learned where she was.

She slid a candle from the stand by the door and lit it with the match she had taken from the dining room at supper. She walked down the long hallway to the stairwell, checking to be sure no one was following. What she was about to do would break the rules, and though she did not know whose rules they were or who would punish her if she was caught, she was sure the penalty would be swift and severe.

Yet she needed to know the truth.

She made her way all the way up to the sewing room, but she hadn't come to see the dress.

Kate's warning from the first night rang in her ears: *"We're not allowed to look outside."*

But Avery didn't care. She moved to the heavily draped window, pausing only briefly before pushing the curtain aside.

Right now Avery cared about only one thing: she needed to know what she could see when she looked outside.

The entire village lay before her like a collection of dollhouse pieces, the houses on the other side of the Salt Sea glowing with warm, golden light while the chimneys produced tiny puffs of smoke. Water inlets snaked through the village like blue veins beneath paper-thin skin.

Though she had never seen the castle before, she wondered—this high off the ground—if she might find anything she recognized. She felt like she was sitting in the clouds.

From the top of the castle, she searched for Murphey's Flower Store and her father's shop—Godfrey's. She also looked for the grocer and the butcher and the masonry, but she couldn't spot them anywhere.

Of course not. Home is so far away.

And then the thought crossed her mind that she had adamantly refused to consider since her first night in the castle. Was it possible that her father, too, was missing—that her entire family was in danger? All this time, Avery had assumed her father was worried about her and Henry. But maybe he didn't even know they were missing. Maybe he was waiting for Avery to search for him.

Could there be truth to what Tuck had said? *"You're sure your father is still alive?"*

She swatted the question away.

"He and Henry are fine," she said aloud. "They are *fine*."

Avery let the drape fall back into place and was heading back to the door when she caught sight of a silhouette on the stairs, heard a rustle that was definitely human. She blew out the candle and dove beneath the wedding dress.

All was quiet, and she wondered if it had been a scout on the stairs. She hoped he hadn't seen her looking out the window. What consequences might there be?

Then, suddenly, two sets of footsteps approached on the marble floor.

"In 'ere you will see the dress. I only 'ope it meets your expectations."

The old woman!

The room filled with light, and a single pair of heels clicked in a lazy circle around the mannequin. Avery held her breath.

"It needs more pearls," came the whine that made Avery's blood run cold. She could have reached out and touched Angelina from where she crouched. "And more diamonds. When I enter the Great Hall, I want to be the brightest thing in the room."

If they moved the dress for any reason, she was a dead girl.

"Yes, ma'am," the old woman said. The dress swayed all around Avery as Angelina tugged at the material.

A third voice added, "Would you like to try it on?"

Avery stiffened. The third voice belonged to Kate.

Kate? How could it be?

"I've seen enough," Angelina snapped. "Now fix it."

Avery waited what seemed a lifetime until she was certain the three were gone before she crawled out and stood, waiting until her legs stopped shaking enough so she could walk back down to her bed.

Where she expected to find Kate's bed empty, instead Kate was fast asleep, snoring lightly.

⌒∞⌒

Time had no meaning in the castle.

Avery began marking her days using the ivory hairpins she borrowed from Kate. Each morning she added one to the edge of her pillow. Today brought the total to six.

Six days more than I ever expected to spend in a real castle.

Six days more than I ever wanted to spend away from home.

Kate brought her a second dress, this one a deep blue with gold hand-stitching, trimmed at the neck with dozens of stunning pearls.

"How do we get to wear dresses like this?" Avery asked over breakfast.

"Thankfully for us, Angelina has a weakness for new gowns and she refuses to wear anything publicly more than once. If she has made an appearance in a dress, she tosses it."

"So how do you get them?"

"The scouts collect them and bring them to the sewing room. We alter them, sometimes making multiple dresses from each one."

Kate was refusing to look her in the eye.

"Did you leave your bed last night?" Avery asked.

"No, but you did," Kate said with a wry smile.

chapter 12

If You Can't Stand the Heat

The girls in the bakery needed help.

With all of the preparations for the wedding under way, they made a formal plea at breakfast for anyone who was able to come. Avery decided she would do what she could, even if that meant just gathering staples for the girls who knew what they were doing. That was better than feeling useless.

She considered helping the cooks, preparing meals for the king, and using the scraps to make meals for the kids. But the king liked to eat steamed dumplings, mincemeat pies, or duck gizzards, and Avery preferred the smell of baked goods to anything that had recently been alive.

She was pleasantly surprised that the bakery girls welcomed her.

They seemed to have the cheerful memory of a gnat.

She was given a tour of the pantry and was led to a small door on the far wall of the kitchen. "It's a dumbwaiter!" one of the girls announced, opening the door with a flourish.

Five pairs of eyes peered inside, their excitement palpable.

Talking enthusiastically over each other, the girls explained that this magical box was controlled by a thick rope on a pulley guided by rails so food could be delivered to all parts of the castle.

The girls were soon buzzing with activity, collecting bowls, spoons, and ingredients for their stations and chatting happily.

Avery distinctly heard the word *election*.

She had heard whispering at breakfast about a mysterious vote and wondered what it was all about. Everyone seemed pleased about it, but she would be as embarrassed admitting she knew nothing about it as she would be revealing her confusion about baking. She didn't want to ruin this second chance with the girls in the kitchen. They were being so kind.

So she didn't ask any questions.

"Do you need help?" one of the girls asked.

Avery should have admitted she needed as much help as a drowning cat, but with everyone in the room seeming to listen to how she would respond, she smiled and said, "No, thank you. I'm doing fine."

Her strategy was simple. She would copy the girl next to her. *How hard can it be?*

Her main goal was to avoid burning down the kitchen. She didn't even need her food to be edible or pretty. She could sneak it into the waste sack before she left. She only wanted to feel accepted—to be part of a group like this one.

She wandered into the staples room, but even as she looked at the bags of sugar and baskets of apples, her mind traveled elsewhere and she couldn't focus.

Maybe the election is a necessary step before going home.

There are easily two hundred apples in this room. Who needs two hundred apples?

What is Angelina doing right now? What secrets does she know about the king?

The girls bustling around the bakery table wouldn't notice she was missing, and Kate wasn't around to tell her she was wrong, so she slipped silently into the darkness of the pantry and knelt, cranking open the slat to peer through the vent.

As he had the first time she had seen him here, the king sat at his desk covered with thick books, stacks of parchment, and piles of private papers. He was talking to a man Avery didn't recognize but assumed was an adviser. The man wore a scarlet robe and a tiny square hat.

"She'll be the downfall of your kingdom," the man said. "Every poor decision you've made in recent days goes back to that woman."

"I have no choice," the king replied between heavy, watery coughs. "I need an heir and she'll provide one."

"But, Your Grace, you have an heir."

With these words, the king flew out of his seat and grabbed the robed man by the throat. "Never say those words aloud again, do you hear me?"

The man nodded, and the king loosened his grip.

He reached for a cloth and coughed into it and Avery saw the unmistakable spread of blood, but neither the king nor the robed man seemed alarmed.

Only when the king sat down did the man continue to speak.

"Forgive me, Your Grace, but if it's about securing a dynasty, you have other options. We could begin a search. I know people from the village who might be able to find him. Or at least give you the peace of mind that he really is dead."

Who's dead? If there's a chance the king's heir is alive, the king wouldn't need to marry Angelina, and maybe we could all go free.

"You know it's more than that," the king was saying when Avery listened again. "Angelina knows *the truth*. She won't rest until she wears the crown. And I won't fight her. We will be married and she will reign beside me."

Bowing slightly, the man in the square hat excused himself from the room.

Moments later, the king followed.

Avery was just about to close the vent when a door on the opposite side of the king's office creaked open and a child—presumably a scout—scurried inside. Moving silently, he went to the king's desk, riffled through a pile of papers, and took only a few that interested him. He set a stack of letters on the chair and grabbed a book from the king's shelf on his way out.

All of this in a matter of seconds.

No sooner had the door closed behind the scout than the opposite door opened and the king returned.

So close!

Avery heard commotion from the baking room and quickly cranked the vent closed.

When she returned with an armload of staples, the kitchen had suddenly cleared, leaving no sign of the girls she had been working with, not to mention the dozens of others who had been coming and going.

"Strange," she mumbled, dumping her ingredients on the table with a thud and wondering if she had missed some obvious reason she was required to leave the room.

And then she heard it.

A voice she recognized right outside the door. Sharp and whiny.

Not again! The kids had fled because Angelina was coming. The bell in the corner of the room must have sounded when she was deep in the pantry.

Everyone else had fled for the stairwell as they were instructed to do.

Avery flew across the room and slid behind the baking table, knees drawn up to her chest. Right above where she hid she saw the reason Angelina was likely on her way into the kitchen: a tall half-iced cake, decorated with hundreds of tiny sugar flowers.

And she knew it was only a matter of seconds until Angelina towered above her.

Once again, the beating of her heart was the loudest thing she heard.

chapter 13

The Wrong Move

Here came that familiar *clack-clack, clack-clack*. This was becoming a habit.

"In 'ere you'll see what we've prepared," the old woman said.

There was nowhere for Avery to go. Judging from the sound of Angelina's heels on the marble floor, the queen-to-be and the old woman stood between Avery and the door.

If they rounded the thick wooden worktable on which the cake sat, they would see her, and everything the kids had worked to protect would be destroyed.

Or *she* would be destroyed.

Or she would be sent to the Forbidden City everyone whispered about.

Bottom line: she wouldn't see her family again.

Avery had one choice. It might not work, but it was better than doing nothing. On her hands and knees, she scurried quickly as the heels moved closer, and at the last instant she leapt into the dumbwaiter and closed the door.

It was a good thing, as the two women came around the table and stood right where she had been hiding.

"At least my cake is almost done," Angelina whined. "Please

tell me it will taste good, or I will cry right here."

Avery suspected Angelina didn't cry as often as she made other people cry.

"It is my sincerest 'ope, ma'am," the old woman said.

"Cut a piece and let me taste it!"

"Of course!"

Folded into a nearly impossible ball, Avery heard the clatter and eventually the verdict.

"Too dry."

"Forgive me," the old woman sputtered, fear in her tone. "You deserve better."

The cake landed in the waste sack with a thud, hours of work coming to a tragic end.

"Must I think of everything?" Angelina droned. "This is why I have a staff. I have a country to run since the king isn't capable of it, and I can't be bothered with dresses and cakes that are unfit for a queen."

"A second cake will be made immediately," the old woman said.

"Yes, it must. And one more thing. . ."

The room grew suddenly quiet, and Avery strained to hear Angelina's voice.

"I want you to go through the staff again, person by person. Leave no one out. Keep everyone you trust and those you don't—"

Discard them, Avery thought.

"I've gone through the staff 'alf a dozen times—"

"Do it again!"

Angelina grunted, the sound of her heels moved in the opposite direction, and the door slammed.

Avery waited until she was sure neither of the women would return. She would wait one more minute before emerging from her cramped hiding place. Taking a deep breath, she rolled her head from side to side, relaxing the muscles that had grown tense during the wait.

And then the unthinkable happened. The dumbwaiter began to move.

Up it went, one jerking motion after another.

Avery didn't know what to do. If she put her arms out to stop the motion, she could break them. If she found a way to lodge the moving cart, she could get stuck in the wall. She could jump, but if she did, she could plunge to a painful death several stories below. For all she knew, the dumbwaiter could be hundreds of feet off the cobblestone ground. No one would even know where to look for her body. If she did manage to climb out, where would she go? She considered calling out for whoever was pulling the ropes to stop. But what if it was an adult and not a kid?

Panic seized her, and she couldn't breathe.

She was right back where she started—on the brink of ruining everything. She seemed to have a talent for it.

Avery closed her eyes and awaited her fate.

The dumbwaiter abruptly halted, and the door opened.

And the voice that greeted her was low and kind. Avery opened her eyes to see Tuck standing there—kind Tuck with the alarming green eyes—hand outstretched.

I have never been so happy to see you, she thought but didn't dare say.

She accepted his hand more eagerly than she otherwise would have and crawled out.

They were adjacent to the kids' dining room.

"How did you know I was in there?" Avery asked.

Tuck smiled. "We have scouts everywhere. As soon as you crawled in, half a dozen of them panicked and came to find me."

Avery's face grew warm. "It wasn't the first time they notified you about me, was it?"

Tuck shook his head slowly. "Not even the first time today. You like to keep the scouts busy." Then more quietly he added, "Be careful, Avery. Life in this castle is no fairy tale. I like your spirit, but you've got to use it for good. We are in a fight for our lives and for the lives of our family members."

Avery saw the face of her little brother and knew Tuck was right.

She also wanted to prove to Tuck that she *was* using her energy for good.

"The king has an heir," Avery blurted. "I heard him tell a man in his office this morning. I think it's the secret everyone keeps whispering about. I'm sure it affects us, but I don't know how."

Avery expected Tuck to disagree with her, but he only smiled.

"The king's heir is no secret. I'm told his first wife, Elizabeth, delivered a baby boy, making the king the happiest man on earth. But hours later both Elizabeth and her son died, and now no one is allowed to talk about it. The king forbids even his closest advisers from discussing it."

Once again, her imagination had gotten the better of her. She did not miss what Tuck said next, a gleam in his eye— "You're here for a reason. Figure out what it is."

chapter 14

The Ballot Box

Avery was sleeping soundly when someone shook her.

At first she thought it was her father, waking her to start the morning chores.

Kate's face slowly swam into focus. "Get up and come with me."

Looking around, Avery saw she was the only one still in bed, and her friend was wearing a beautiful dress instead of a nightgown.

"How did I oversleep?"

"I'll help you get dressed. Come on." Kate tugged on Avery's arm until Avery finally swung her legs over the side of the mattress and stood.

Her head pounded and her stomach clenched. "I think I'm sick."

Kate laughed. "No, you're not. It's midnight. You're just tired." She held out a dress—black cotton velvet with panels of gold. "Put this on. It'll look good with your hair."

"I hate to disappoint you, but nobody is going to notice my hair. And why do you keep bringing me clothes? One of these dresses would have lasted me a lifetime at home."

"Just put it on," Kate said with a laugh. "Are you always this difficult?"

"Why are we getting dressed when we should be sleeping?"

"You'll see."

Kate helped Avery finish fastening the gown then pushed Avery into a chair and began combing her hair with a heavy, gold-plated hairbrush that made Avery wince with each stroke.

"Tell me something I don't know about you," Kate said as she worked.

"My mother disappeared two years ago."

"Oh?"

"She kissed me one morning when I was playing with Henry in the woods and said she would see me soon. She reminded me not to lose my ruby flower necklace, and then she left and never came back."

"I'm sorry," Kate said. "I'm sure that was painful."

"I've never known any pain like it until I lost Henry. He was my responsibility after my mother disappeared, and I failed him."

Kate stopped brushing. "You haven't lost Henry. I know you have questions, and we will find the answers together. I'm on your side, always."

Avery turned and looked at Kate. "The other night I was almost asleep when I heard you say you would help me find them if I stayed here. What did you mean?"

Kate's eyes darkened. "I *will* help you, but I'm sure you were only dreaming."

Not a moment too soon, Kate was done and held up a mirror. Avery laughed in shocked delight.

Her once-unruly nest had been brushed to a shine and was pulled back into a series of braids that met in a knot at the base of her neck. She looked years older and felt prettier than she thought possible.

"Who taught you to do this?" Avery asked, but Kate was already tugging her arm.

"We need to go! We're late."

⸎

Kate led Avery to a huge meeting hall where she could almost taste the excitement in the air. A group in the center of the room bobbed for apples. Others ate popcorn balls or tossed bags of beans at wooden pins, cheering when they knocked them all down. There was laughter and music instead of the normal hushed tones and sideways glances. Even the boys who fought every morning at the breakfast table appeared to be getting along.

Everyone wore festive clothes—several girls wore wreaths of green leaves and red berries in their hair. A table was laden with more treats than could possibly be eaten by everyone in the room. A heavy chandelier bore hundreds of candles that set the room ablaze in gold.

From this perspective, the kids' side of the castle was a kingdom unto itself.

"What's going on?" Avery called. "Won't we be discovered?"

"The king is throwing a large banquet downstairs to celebrate his new engagement. It will last all hours of the night. Scouts are on guard to be sure we are safe."

Avery pulled Kate to a corner where she could hear herself over the din.

"So what are *we* celebrating?" she shouted.

"Tonight is the election!"

"What is the election? Will it help us get out of here?"

"You've got to stop trying to get out of here and start figuring out why you're here in the first place."

Kate nudged Avery in the direction of a boy in a corner distributing small pieces of parchment. He tapped a large wooden box and said in a rehearsed, if not overly enthusiastic voice, "Voting is a sacred privilege, ladies. Write the name of the person you feel is best suited to lead us and cast your vote into this box. Remember, your decision could alter our destiny." He bowed dramatically.

Avery rolled her eyes.

She had thought the vote was important—something related to the king or even their freedom—but this was just a silly stunt the kids created to distract themselves. It was nothing more than voting for the leader of their little secret society.

Kate smiled. "Two ballots, please."

It seemed a waste of time, but Avery wrote a name in large black letters and dropped it into the box. She intended to make a sarcastic remark, but Kate yanked her to a table of apple bars, warm from the oven.

"Rumor has it," Kate said, "that you don't know how to bake."

"No idea what you're talking about," Avery said with a smile.

❦

The party continued long into the night before the music stopped and Ballot Box Boy called everyone together. Avery nicknamed him Boxy in her mind.

"Leadership is important," Boxy began. "It is vital that someone rise up from among us and lead this group as our junior king. Our corner of the castle needs a leader that is better than any downstairs."

The crowd erupted.

Avery was annoyed that the kids seemed to take the vote so seriously. This wasn't a real election. It had no consequences. Junior kings were powerless.

Boxy continued. "Never believe the lie that we can't be leaders. It's a myth circulated by adults who choose not to lead. Even as kids we have everything we need to make an impact on other people."

Again the kids broke into applause, and Avery wondered if Boxy himself hoped to be king.

"Two weeks ago," Boxy said, "we agreed we should elect our own king, responsible to guide our search for freedom. I hold in my hand the results."

The crowd leaned forward in anticipation.

chapter 15

Coronation

With great gusto, Boxy unfolded the parchment and held it high for everyone to see.

"You have elected Tuck to be our king!"

Avery forgot her annoyance and joined in the applause. She, too, had voted for Tuck. There was something undeniably *leader-like* about him.

Kate leaned close and whispered, "You're obviously happy about this."

Avery didn't have time to respond before Tuck was prodded forward. He looked embarrassed as Boxy presented him with a heavy gold medallion to wear around his neck and a thick fur shawl that looked several sizes too big and seemed to weigh him down. Avery wondered if these, too, had been castle castoffs. They looked like something a prince would wear.

They look right on Tuck.

The crowd quieted and Boxy held out a book that looked like an old atlas. Tuck put his hand on it before Boxy began to speak. "Will you promise to rule us according to the laws and customs we create with justice and mercy in all your decisions?"

"I will."

"Then I proudly declare you our junior king."

The crowd erupted again, calling for Tuck to say something.

After trying to quiet them, he turned a wooden bucket upside down and stood on it so that he was head and shoulders above everyone.

"Thank you," he said as the kids clapped and whistled and called out their congratulations. A few yelled, "We knew it!" and pumped their fists.

"Until today," Tuck said, "we've each played by our own rules. We were each brought here against our will, and we've each handled it in our own way. But look around. We're all here for the same reason, but what have we done to make our situation better? How have we worked together to accomplish good? Are we any closer to freedom now than the day we arrived?"

A collective *no* rose from the crowd.

"Today, everything changes. Today we set aside our tribal rivalries and personal ambitions to become a family. I will do my best to lead honorably. I will carry your hope and your confidence with me. You can depend on that."

A cheer went up.

Avery could see in that moment why everyone admired Tuck.

Tuck continued. "I need to depend on you to promise to do your best to love your neighbor as yourself. And you have my word, I will find a way for us all to be free as soon as possible."

Avery wondered what *free* meant to orphans. While they may have felt this was the first place they had a large extended family, it couldn't last forever. Either they would be turned back out to fend for themselves on the street or they would be *discarded*. Angelina's words rang in her mind.

"I will kill. . . All. Of. Them."

The faces in the room—dirty, tired, and sad—were those of kids who hadn't had a mother to tell them stories or a father to build them tree houses. Even held captive in a castle, Avery knew she had been more blessed in her lifetime than anyone else in the room.

Boxy was talking again.

"Tuck, it is now your duty to select a cabinet of two you can rely on to help you do your job—an adviser and a queen. Choose wisely."

Tuck didn't hesitate. "For adviser, Kendrick," he said, motioning for a wiry, bespectacled, unsmiling boy who appeared uncomfortable as he stood to join Tuck.

"He was the one who arrived the day you did," Kate whispered.

The boy in the other box on the raft.

He was solemn and scholarly. The choice surprised Avery, but she suspected Tuck had the charisma and Kendrick had the intellect to form a strong team.

Boxy presented Kendrick with a smaller medallion to wear around his neck.

And then a sinking feeling hit Avery. She knew who would be queen. Ilsa sat a few feet away, giggling with a group of girls who were already patting her on the back and whispering in her ear.

She'd been campaigning for Tuck's nomination for king all along—with her own appointment in mind, of course. It all made sense now.

Tuck raised a hand to quiet the buzz over Kendrick's selection. "And for queen..."

No one moved.

"I choose Avery."

The crowd gasped.

The clapping—what little there was—proved short-lived and felt forced.

"Who?"

"Who's Avery?"

"The girl who almost burned down the kitchen?"

The questions weren't even subtle. Avery could hear them from where she sat.

And she couldn't blame them.

She was as surprised as they were. She hardly knew anyone but Kate, and she had no interest in staying in the castle any longer than she had to, let alone in being part of some secret cabinet led by kids in the castle of a king who ordered them *discarded*.

The kids looked around expectantly.

Kate nudged her and whispered, "You really need to stand. Tuck is waiting."

Knowing her face had to be pulsing crimson, Avery shuffled to her feet and moved through a silent crowd to join Tuck and Kendrick. She owed Tuck that much. He was being kind to her *again*.

She would argue his decision later, encourage him to make Kate his queen.

Boxy handed Tuck a tiara made of perfect pink pearls—

simple yet beautiful—and Avery was grateful, suddenly, that her hair was fixed.

Kate knew I would be elected, but how?

Avery knelt, and Tuck placed the tiara on her head. Avery wondered what royal had worn it. It was nothing like the crowns of sticks she had worn in the woods.

Boxy formally intoned, "Tuck, Avery, and Kendrick, wear your adornments with pride, as they indicate you accept the responsibility they represent. If you should ever choose to resign your post, you must forfeit these tokens."

Avery wanted to remove the tiara and run for the door, but when she caught sight of Ilsa—surrounded by her black-ribboned ladies in waiting, her mouth set and her eyes fixed on Avery's—she decided the tiara would stay right where it was for the time being.

In fact, she met Ilsa's gaze and reached with both hands to straighten the tiara and make sure it was firmly in place.

Fiddle playing erupted from the corner and the kids began clapping and dancing—dresses twirling under the swaying chandelier—every worry seeming momentarily forgotten.

I must be the only one who doesn't want to be here, trapped in this perfect world.

To me, a world without my family is the farthest thing from perfect.

On the other hand, a growing friendship with Tuck was nice.

⁂

"You should have been made queen," Avery said to Kate that night in the darkness of their bunk room. "You know more about castle life than I do, and you're good at it. You *look* the part."

"I don't want it," Kate replied. "The life of a queen is not to be envied. Her responsibilities are outnumbered only by her enemies."

"What are you saying?"

"Watch your back, Avery."

chapter 16

The Threat

The next morning, Avery was tying the laces on her dress when Ilsa appeared, and the rest of the bunk room emptied. *Of course,* Avery thought, as Ilsa crossed her arms and narrowed her eyes.

Avery had expected this confrontation, but not necessarily so soon.

"I'm going to let you in on a little secret," Ilsa began. "You know Tuck made you queen because you can't do anything else, right? Everyone's been talking about how useless you are around here, almost burning down the kitchen, getting stuck in the wall, and failing everything else you've tried. Tuck took pity on you because he's that kind of a boy. Always too nice."

"Maybe you could take a lesson from him," Avery said quietly.

Ilsa laughed. "You have no idea what you're talking about."

"I'm sure you'll educate me."

"The point is, you stole the election from me just like you tried stealing my bed your first night here. Like you're trying to steal Tuck now."

"I haven't stolen anything from you."

"Right." Ilsa came so close that Avery backed against the cold wall. No one was close enough to rescue her if she called for help, and who would risk Ilsa's rage anyway? Ilsa brought her face so close that Avery could smell the morning coffee on her breath. "This isn't over. Not by a long shot. Stay away from Tuck. Understand?"

"We don't need to be enemies. We can work together."

"We can?" Ilsa asked in mock surprise. She clasped her heart. "You could be the beauty and I could be the brains." She narrowed her eyes. "Oh wait. You couldn't be either one!" Ilsa laughed. "You are so slow. I didn't decide we were enemies. You did. And now I will destroy you with any means at my disposal. And just so you're aware, I win whatever battles I fight." Ilsa tightened her grip on Avery's arm. "Understand?"

Avery nodded, afraid of what Ilsa might do to her arm if she disagreed.

Ilsa turned to leave then turned back. "I can have you sent to the Forbidden City. Remember that."

That was the umpteenth time Avery had heard talk of this mysterious place.

As soon as Ilsa was gone, the bunk room filled again as if nothing had happened.

Everyone fears Ilsa.

Worse than the threat, worse even than the prospect of the Forbidden City—whatever that entailed—was that Avery feared Ilsa was right. Tuck had chosen her as queen solely out of pity. Or maybe he thought giving her the role would keep her out of trouble. Either way, she would wear the tiara only until the first meeting of the cabinet. Then she would tell Tuck to give it to someone else. She didn't want Ilsa to have it, but accepting the role just to upset her didn't make sense. She needed to avoid the Forbidden City at all costs.

⚬∞⚬

After breakfast, Avery led Kate down the stone stairwell, whispering, "You aren't the only one who is allowed to learn the secrets of this place."

Kate looked hesitant.

"The king and Angelina are away today."

Kate stopped walking. "So?"

"I want to see what I can discover in the hundreds of rooms on the other side from where we live," Avery told her. "Since it's my job to assist Tuck in leadership, no one will be suspicious if I'm gone for a while."

Avery had prepared an excuse in case she was questioned by Tuck. She was looking for grates in each of the rooms so she could find a way to track Angelina on her own. Maybe tracking Angelina would lead her to Henry or to information that would prove valuable for their freedom.

Maybe it would lead her to so much more.

chapter 17

The Discovery

According to the stories Avery's mother had told, the castle sat atop an intricate system of tunnels that traveled various outlets within the village. Rumor had it that the largest of all snaked its way under the Salt Sea and ended within the walls of a tiny, beautiful chapel in the village.

"Even royalty knows that God exists among the humble," her mother had said.

Learning where all the outlets were might prove useful in helping the kids escape.

Stop one: the Great Hall.

Kate and Avery stood in the doorway, their jaws hanging open and their eyes wide, taking in thirteen chandeliers, each the width of Avery's bedroom at home. Each bore hundreds of candles that flickered and danced, throwing shadows on the opulent golden ceiling and casting a reverent glow on the throne in the center of the room.

It sat eerily empty this morning, adorned with the royal arms of the kingdom.

"There'll soon be another throne beside it," Kate said. "The boys upstairs are building Angelina's now. I've seen it."

"I wonder what the king would think if he knew it was being built by the orphans he has sentenced to death. I wonder how he would react if he knew his *entire castle* rested on the shoulders of kids."

"The wedding will take place right here," Kate said, and Avery had to admit this news excited her, in spite of everything. It was an excuse to be happy about something, even if only for a day.

The only weddings she had attended were ones where country girls wore their one church dress and threaded daisies in their hair before heading to the chapel where a few family members waited. She had watched dozens of girls marry at fifteen or sixteen and had always assumed she would be one of them.

Her father had recently made it clear that it was time she started thinking about it. He hinted at this every time he instructed her to clean house or prepare supper or watch Henry.

"You must learn to do these things for yourself," he would say, and Avery knew what he meant. But none of the boys in their village interested her. Their chief concern was catching frogs or building forts out of river rocks.

She wanted something more—something better.

Now she wondered whether she would ever marry at all.

"Someone's coming!" Kate said, grabbing Avery's arm and yanking her to a spot behind a huge oak door. They stood huddled together—neither of them daring to breathe—until a staff member passed and was long gone.

Stop number two: the Hall of Mirrors—used by the queen to make sure her dresses were precisely what she wanted. It was exactly as it sounded—floor-to-ceiling mirrors.

Avery wished the hall could talk. It would have much to say about the dozens of queens through the ages who had fussed and snapped, clapped and praised.

She imagined hundreds of dressmakers had scurried in silence, conceding to demands and pleading for their lives when a stray button or crooked hem had left the queen wanting.

Avery quickly understood that for every discovery she made within the castle walls, hundreds more waited to be uncovered.

She ran ahead of Kate down the endless hall, her braid flying behind her and her slippered footsteps falling silently on the white marble. For a few minutes at least, she forgot why she was in the castle and remembered only that she was thirteen. She twirled and admired her elegant dress in the mirrors. It was the first time she had seen herself—head to toe—attired this way. She knew her mother would be pleased.

Gone was the dirty-faced, wild-haired child.

Next, they visited the chapel, with its stunning gold-gilded walls and stained-glass windows that cast a rosy hue. High-back pews were separated by a center aisle, carpeted in crimson, leading to an intricately carved pulpit of dark, rich wood.

"No one in the royal family uses this chapel," Kate said, "so some of us who are thirteen use it when we can. You should join us."

Avery did not respond. It was difficult to think about worshipping God when so many things were going wrong. *Or maybe,* she thought, *this is the most important time to pray.*

She would consider it.

The final room they came to was near the center of the castle, filled with every piece of furniture imaginable, buried beneath thick, dusty quilts covered with a fine layer of dust.

Kate and Avery swatted away cobwebs and began peeking beneath blankets and lifting lids off boxes. At first they were timid, but soon they jumped with joy at each discovery.

They found ornate paintings and beautiful rugs, a stunning harp and several tall mirrors. They found brass bed frames, ancient vases, and bundles of handwritten letters tied with faded ribbons. They discovered silver candlesticks they suspected were worth more than country houses. They unearthed boxes of jewelry and jeweled hairpieces that made them squeal.

"These were worn by queens!" Avery said, twirling with a set of ivory combs.

Avery's mind raced. Why were they sleeping, working, and playing in rooms virtually bare when all of this existed in storage a few hundred feet from where they lived?

She would show Tuck.

Of course, that would mean she would need the courage to actually approach him. Even looking at him made her nervous lately.

"We should go," Kate said. "We've seen enough for one day."

Avery wanted to protest. *Is that even possible?*

The castle contained enough rooms to fill a month of exploring—maybe more.

And I still need to find the tunnels.

Avery caught sight of a painting framed in gold leaf and half hidden beneath a blanket. She saw just enough of a woman's face—smooth and exotic—to compel her to see more. She took a few careful steps over stacks of fragile china and crates of marble then pulled the blanket far enough down to bring the face into view.

Beautiful eyes, distinct as they could be, one blue and the other brown.

Impossible. Avery tried to shove the thought aside.

One of her mother's songs came flooding back:

She walks the endless corridors, she dances through the halls,
She sings of better days gone by, and laughs at cannonballs,
She's known not by the crown that rests upon her golden head,
But by her eyes, for one is brown; the other's blue instead.

"This is the queen," Avery whispered.

"What did you say?" Kate asked, coming to stand beside her.

"This must be the king's first wife. *She* must be Queen Elizabeth!"

Kate didn't respond.

"I bet everything in this room belonged to her," Avery continued. "After she died, the king must have moved all of her things into this room."

"We really need to go back to our quarters," Kate said. "Let's go."

The king and Angelina are keeping the first queen's secrets. What on earth could they be? And what if we could find the answers in this room?

The treasures in the room whispered for her to stay.

"You go ahead," Avery said. "I'll be right there."

"Don't be long," Kate said as she left. "I'm sure we're not supposed to be in here."

Avery nodded, never taking her eyes off the painting, the blanket now bunched beneath the woman's chin. As soon as Kate was out of sight, Avery yanked the blanket entirely away. And when she did, what she saw made her blood go cold.

The queen was wearing a necklace with a large ruby flower.

chapter 18

King versus Queen

At her first cabinet meeting, Avery found Tuck deep in conversation, appointing kids one at a time to important castle duties.

"You are now Junior Keeper of the Great Seal," he said to a boy who beamed.

Is there truly such a thing?

The line of kids waiting to talk to Tuck was at least twenty deep; and of course, he was speaking kindly to each one of them, making every person feel valued and needed.

"We'll be here all day," Avery said, flopping into a chair at the table beside Kendrick.

Kendrick didn't look up from signing his way through a mountain of paperwork. He had perfected the signatures of several castle dignitaries and was able to sign important deeds without hesitation.

"It's what we agreed to do," he said.

Avery's hand went to the ruby necklace that now seemed to weigh a thousand pounds around her neck. After seeing it in the painting of Queen Elizabeth, she kept it hidden beneath her dress or buried in her pillow. Being caught with royal jewels was punishable by death. She wondered, though, how her mother had come to own the necklace and why she had given it away. Her mother was growing as mysterious to her as the castle had become.

"Hello," Tuck said finally, when the line had cleared. "We have a lot to do. Let's get started." His voice was gentle and his eyes were kind.

As he spoke about the kids and the responsibilities of the council to meet their needs, Avery tried not to notice that his eyes twinkled or that he seemed to genuinely like the people he served. He assigned Kendrick to intercept the daily mail coming to and going from the castle so they could become more familiar with the goings-on of the king. And he charged Avery with designing "a crest, a unifying emblem—something we can rally around."

Avery nodded, smiling.

Maybe she had finally found a place where her gifts would be useful.

He then talked for the next hour or so about the complexities of parliamentary process and the details of domestic and foreign policy, but Avery didn't hear a word he said.

And that was just fine with her.

⤜∞⤛

Late that night, Tuck introduced a new activity. The kids met in the large hall on their side of the stairwell for chess tournaments. Winners would receive passes from chores like dishwashing and mopping, while losers would be assigned the most mundane tasks.

The tension was intense from the moment the pairings were announced and the players began arranging their pieces.

Winners were treated like heroes.

Losers sulked until bedtime.

Brawls often broke out, especially among the boys, until someone—usually Tuck—broke them up and sent the rivals in opposite directions to cool off.

Two boys lost teeth, their bloody gums less of a concern than their ruined brackets.

When the kids weren't playing chess, they were discussing strategies and making plans.

Breakfast gossip generally revolved around the previous evening's results.

Friendships were forged or frayed over a single tournament.

The best moments of the day were when the kids were deep into their matches, tensions high and moods volatile. A single move across the checkered board could result in half a dozen bloody lips or swollen eyes by lights-out. More than one board was swept clean by the forearm of an angry opponent.

Avery enjoyed the matches so much that when she was watching she actually liked living in the castle—felt like she belonged.

⟡

Late one night, several weeks since she'd arrived at the castle, Avery stood watching a pair of players arrange their pieces in preparation for a game.

"Do you play?" a voice behind her asked.

She turned to see Tuck and shook her head.

"I find it interesting," he said, his voice low, "that the king is the most prized and protected piece, yet also one of the weakest."

Avery smiled, remembering the king giving in to Angelina's demands for a marriage proposal. But Kate had been adamant that they not mention it to anyone, so she didn't share this thought with Tuck.

A signal was given and the children began poring over their boards, chess pieces clanking as pawns were collected.

"Rumor has it," Tuck said quietly, "the king is dying."

Avery looked at Tuck in confusion.

"Everything he is doing right now—including his plan to marry—is because he needs an heir. Time is of the essence. If he dies with no legitimate heir, his name will die with him."

"There are worse things," Avery whispered.

"Not for a king."

A question burned on the edges of Avery's mind, and she wasn't sure she had the courage to voice it. She had already made a fool of herself so many times in Tuck's presence.

"Tuck, what if the king's first son didn't die?"

"Then he'd be next in line to the throne."

"No," Avery pressed. "What I meant is—what if the king's son is alive?"

Tuck didn't respond, but it was clear he was thinking about it as they moved from game to game, following the tournament well into the night. When Avery finally excused herself to go to her room, Tuck asked, "Did you notice the queen is the most powerful piece on the board?"

She smiled but did not turn around.

In chess, at least, it's because the queen never rules with her heart. She, however, did not have that luxury.

She knew it was time to find the courage to talk to Tuck alone.

chapter 19

Pinned

Avery sat in the bunk room with her slender reeds of charcoal and blocks of colored chalk, staring at blank sheets of sketch paper. They were the nicest tools she had ever been given. Yet for days, she had been unable to draw.

Once she had no supplies with an endless source of inspiration.

Now she had the very best supplies with no vision.

It had been too long since she had breathed fresh air, heard leaves crunch, or smelled the smoke of a crackling bonfire. She wanted so badly to hear the snap of clean laundry on a clothesline or to see the face of her silly, dumb dog.

She was beginning to forget her mother's voice.

She wondered how much older Henry looked. Little boys could grow up overnight.

Give her the perfect spot under one of her trees and she could create a dozen sketches by evening. But on a borrowed mattress in an empty room in a cold castle—

She threw her sketch paper into the air.

I want to go home.

Her small house had a wide cobblestone walk in front and an unreliable garden in back where her father spent his evenings tending his vegetables obsessively and training his carrier pigeons for who knew what purpose. Wherever her father and brother were, she prayed they were safe. She prayed, too, that God would help her complete the crest. For whatever reason, Tuck believed in her, and she didn't want to fail him.

She picked up a piece of sketch paper and tried again.

"There is a shield in every family crest," her father had told her.

Avery had been bored by his random history lessons back then, but now she wished she had asked more questions.

She drew the shield with small, careful strokes.

"Every crest represents what the family loves," he had said.

So she drew green and yellow butternut tree leaves—dozens of them—sprouting from the shield. In the center she outlined the perfect dark cherry tree, the kind her father used to build clocks or shelves or furniture in his shop.

Next, she drew swirling ribbons through the leaves that extended from the shield, representing her mother's love of sewing. She could still hear the whisper of the fabrics she brought home, could see her mother in the corner late into the evening hand-stitching a work shirt for her father or a dress for one of her father's customers.

"Every crest has a motto."

At the base of the shield, Avery drew a thick, swirling sash on which she wrote, *Viam inveniam aut faciam.* "I will either find a way or make one."

She added a few more swirls of color, protected the drawing between two blank pages of parchment, and made her way up to the sewing room where she would ask Kate to sew it for her.

Late that night, after observing another adrenaline-charged chess tournament, Avery changed into her nightgown. She tore twelve eight-inch strips from cloth Kate had given her and tied sections of her hair against her head as tightly as she could.

As she worked, Kate chirped enthusiastically about Angelina's wedding gown and how perfectly it had all come together. "We will transport it down to her chambers early tomorrow morning with the help of the old woman. I think the king will be pleased with it."

"But will Angelina?"

"Does it matter?" Kate asked with a grin. "She'll be so happy with everyone's hugs and kisses, she won't care what she's wearing."

And suddenly an idea struck Avery.

Once Kate excused herself to take a bath, Avery moved quickly. On a leftover piece of sketch paper, she wrote a simple message with a piece of chalk, folded it, and slipped back upstairs to the empty sewing room. Moving quickly, she pulled the top of the wedding dress bodice down to where it would hit Angelina's collarbone. Carefully, she fastened the note into the dress, sliding a straight pin through the inside of the material, allowing the point to protrude just enough that Angelina wouldn't notice until it was pressed hard against her.

It was a long shot, but if Angelina didn't discover the message until she was in the Great Hall on the afternoon of her wedding day, Avery might be able to assess her role in the kids' captivity.

How the new queen would respond to the message could

reveal everything.

How Avery would ever sleep with such an important day ahead, she had no idea.

chapter 20

The Moment

Avery awoke to excited voices. Today the king would marry Angelina.

The kids' quarters pulsed with anticipation.

Every girl donned her best dress and—for the first time since Avery had arrived at the castle—slippers. Circles of girls stood admiring their feet. The room came alive with the lending of lace and beads, jewelry and ribbons. In the shiniest satin and the softest velvet, it was hard to remember that these were orphans who had been torn from everything they'd known.

Girls took turns helping each other tie sashes or fix hair, and nobody argued about anything. Even Ilsa seemed content at the breakfast table, her posse of ladies giggling all around her.

Everyone chose to dress in his or her finest, even knowing no one else would see them. The boys even washed their hair, leaving trails of water trickling down their temples.

The closest any of them would come to the wedding would be the metal grates the scouts used to track the king. Kids had already staked their claims, announcing which grates they intended to use, bartering for the best during chess tournaments.

A mousy boy with tousled hair and a face full of freckles

had claimed the best grate in the castle after winning an intense round of chess the night before, and he made a huge show of presenting it to Kate one night at supper.

"Would you be so kind as to accept the grate, my lady?" the boy had asked, bowing low as the kids chortled all around him.

Kate was gracious—of course she was—though Avery was confident she had never noticed the boy before and likely would never notice him again. Kate had given no indication of interest in any of the boys. Late at night when girls whispered about their affections for various ones—shifting almost as frequently as they changed their hairstyles—Kate stayed out of it.

❧

Generally speaking, the kids were thrilled about the marriage of the king because they were convinced Angelina would be the answer to their problems.

"She'll help the king see that he's wrong to discard us," Avery heard one of the girls say.

Another said, "When she becomes a mother, she'll understand how important kids are for the kingdom—even kids who don't have families."

One of the wiser girls said, "There are no throwaways in God's kingdom."

They have no idea what they're talking about. Angelina isn't anyone's solution.

Avery thought back to the conversation she had heard her second day in the castle.

"Marry me and make it permanent," Angelina had said.

"Or what?" the king responded.

"Or I will kill. . . All. Of. Them."

Avery knew with certainty things were about to get much worse with Angelina on the throne.

⌘

"Sit," Kate said, smiling, and Avery flopped onto the mattress.

Carefully, Kate went to work untying the pieces of cloth in Avery's hair until each section fell to her shoulders in a picture-perfect coil. Kate tugged and poked and sighed in what sounded to Avery like mock frustration. She was used to it. Her mother had done the same.

When Kate finally released her to the mirror, Avery was pleased. Once again, Kate had worked her magic. Avery's hair was pulled up in an elegant twist, supported by at least a dozen hairpins. Her mother would have been thrilled.

And then there was the dress.

Kate had described it as "green silk taffeta," but that hardly did the gown justice. It caught rays of light from the candles and shimmered like the ruby now hidden in Avery's pillow. It made Avery's dark hair look glossy and elegant, and she almost felt it was *her* day and not Angelina's.

"Where did you learn to do this?" Avery asked.

Kate shrugged, coming to stand beside her. "We each have our secrets."

"I wish you would tell me yours."

"Someday," Kate said with a smile. "I promise."

Avery turned to Kate and held out a slim red ribbon she had cut from a bolt she had taken from storage and been saving for the right moment. "For your wrist."

When Kate hesitated, looking puzzled, Avery pulled her own sleeve up so Kate could see a matching red ribbon on her wrist.

Kate smiled and didn't just tie the ribbon in place, but also knotted it.

And it was then that Avery noticed.

The star on Kate's wrist is gone.

Avery grabbed Kate's arm and pointed to the bare spot. "Where did it go?"

Kate looked confused.

"Your star. It's missing. Mine won't come off no matter how hard I scrub."

"Silly Avery," Kate said, easing her arm out of Avery's grip. "You are so dramatic." She patted Avery's cheek. "It's one of the things I love most about you."

But she didn't answer the question.

⚬⚭⚬

By the time they made it to the grate Kate's secret admirer had bestowed on her (and was too shy to ask to share), Avery was nearly floating. The slats overlooked the very spot where the wedding vows would be exchanged and the angle allowed a perfect panoramic view.

The throne room in the Great Hall swelled with prewedding activity.

The walnut floors had been buffed to a shine. Enormous flower arrangements stood sentinel in elaborate pots throughout a sea of candles that could burn a city in seconds. The fragrance of sweet vanilla wafted up through the vents. The thirteen chandeliers cast a beautiful glow over a makeshift platform, and a ruby-red carpet cut a path from the door where the guests entered to the stage where the ceremony would take place.

According to Kate, the king commissioned the platform so every guest would have an unobstructed view. Avery suspected it was Angelina—and not the king—who insisted on the platform. Angelina needed to be seen.

Supposedly the king—but more likely the queen-to-be—had appointed the castle staff to sew hundreds of festive silk flags and hang them for everyone to see. But naturally this task had eventually found its way to the hidden kids, and Tuck had assigned it to Avery, who reassigned it to Kate.

Now the kingdom was buzzing about the "talented seamstress from the castle."

Avery was proud of her mysterious friend.

Shoulder to shoulder over the grate in their festive dresses, Avery and Kate watched the throne room fill—elaborately dressed adults carrying expensive gifts and talking excitedly as they gathered around long wooden tables bearing platters of fruit and tall silver cups of drink.

Clusters of unmarried girls with intricate braids did their best to draw attention to themselves, as bachelors, in formal attire and carefully polished boots with gleaming buckles, passed seemingly unaware.

The older attendees wore hats bearing large, bright feathers.

Kate and Avery pointed and laughed at the dozen or so plotlines unfolding in the Great Hall beneath them. Every guest had a story.

"I've never seen so many happy people in one place," Avery said. "It's like heaven on earth."

"Don't be fooled," Kate responded. "The Great Hall is always filled with threats."

❦

Even knowing it made no sense, Avery found herself searching carefully for any sign of someone she might recognize. Her father never would have been invited to an occasion like this, but maybe one of his friends or customers might come. Seeing anyone from her village would be an enormous comfort.

She searched each face in vain.

The only person she recognized was the old woman, who looked unusually nice today in a pale dress and matching hat. She stood closer to the stage than Avery would have suspected, and she smiled on occasion.

Avery knew that just outside the gate, throngs of penniless celebrants and packs of hungry kids would be waiting like pigeons to peck at the banquet crumbs. She could already hear the roar of the crowd eagerly anticipating the day.

Maybe her father was among them.

"Hope is the greatest gift we have," her mother had always said.

Avery was finally beginning to understand.

A children's choir began to sing—their perfect treble voices blending as one.

Whispers tore through the crowd as a glowing Angelina appeared in the ivory silk dress with the tiny pearls that shimmered in the light of the sea of candles. She wore a heavy headpiece with a thick veil that covered her face, and she held the arm of a pudgy, gray-haired man Avery assumed was her father. They traversed the crimson-carpeted aisle to take their place on the makeshift stage.

Trumpets blared and everyone turned as the king marched in, wearing a heavy fur robe, broad gold medallion, and gaudy jeweled crown. He also wore a thick belt and heavy boots. Flanked by spear-bearing guards, neither they nor he showed a hint of a smile as they marched to center stage to join Angelina.

Thump, thump, thump, thump.

It sounded to Avery more like a battle procession than a wedding march.

The guests bowed deeply as the king passed.

The ceremony was conducted by a man in a tall, funny hat. He welcomed the guests and spoke happily for several minutes of the king and Angelina. Soon, he invited the couple to kneel and take their vows as cloaks of royal purple were draped around their shoulders.

The king took his vow first.

"I do take thee to be my wedded wife, to have and to hold from this day forward, for better for worse, for richer for poorer, in sickness and in health, till death us do part, and thereto I plight thee my troth."

Avery suspected the words *for poorer* were mere ceremony. And *till death us do part* was something he could arrange, if necessary.

Angelina made her vows, and the man with the funny hat proclaimed them married.

The throne room erupted in thunderous applause as the new couple rose and linked arms. And the kids—from each of their grates—dropped handfuls of white feathers that fell like snow onto the unsuspecting crowd.

Avery heard the roar from the throng of visitors outside. A chorus of cathedral bells sounded, and for a moment, all was right in the world because everyone was happy.

To the apparent delight of the crowd, the king pulled Angelina hard into a more informal embrace, and the new queen's eyes suddenly went wide. The people roared with laughter when she quickly pushed the king away, then they gasped when she clutched herself just below the collarbone with a pained expression.

And suddenly, Avery remembered what she had done.

Angelina reached inside her dress and yanked out a small piece of folded parchment.

Time, for Avery, stood still.

chapter 21

Poison!

"What is going on?" Kate whispered. "What was in her dress?"

Avery did not—*could not*—respond. She could barely breathe.

Like everyone else, she watched Angelina unfold the parchment and read. Of course, only Avery knew what the queen saw, written in chalk:

You have secrets I will uncover if you do not let us go.

The new queen's eyes never narrowed, her brow never furrowed. She did not share the note with her new husband who stood beside her or with one of her ladies who stepped forward to see what Angelina needed. She did not appear at all confused by the words. She merely folded the note, tucked it back into her dress, and smiled—sending chills up Avery's spine.

"She knows we're here," Avery whispered.

"How on earth do you know that?" Kate asked.

When Avery didn't respond, Kate reached across the grate and clutched her wrist. "Why do you think she knows we're here?"

"When you're ready to tell me what you know, I'll tell you what I know."

Kate let go of Avery's wrist, but she did not drop her gaze until the king called—

"And now we feast!"

⁓∞⁓

An hour later, the girls remained at their grate, watching the guests dine enthusiastically on every imaginable delicacy. The guests appeared happy, and the room only fell silent when the king stood. Avery knew, even before the king uttered his first word, that the speech would be filled with the expected platitudes.

A king, after all, belongs to his people.

"Thank you for celebrating with me on the greatest day of my life. You have given Angelina and me the great gift of your presence, and so I would like to offer a gift to you—an announcement you will be the first to hear."

The crowd cheered in anticipation of this declaration.

"I hold this kingdom and everyone in it dear to my heart. Which is why it brings me great joy to announce that I will host the first ever Olympiad very soon. People will travel far and wide to attend the greatest games on earth, right here in our kingdom. It is my way of honoring you and celebrating my new bride."

The Great Hall broke into a thunderous round of applause as the king lifted Angelina's hand and pressed a kiss against her knuckles.

"No expense will be spared! We will hire the best and brightest to build a stadium. Tentmakers will line the streets with colorful expressions of their creativity. We will all be the happiest we have ever been!"

Suddenly the air was punctuated by a shriek, and the crowd turned to see a young man not four feet from Angelina stagger backward, horror spreading over his face. Blood trickled from his nose and ears and streamed down his neck, pooling on his shirt.

"Poison!" someone yelled, and the room filled with screams.

Guards closed in on the king and queen as the young man was yanked from the room and the crowds parted like the Red Sea as shock and fear rippled through the place.

"Did he try to kill the queen?" Avery asked.

Kate shook her head. "He was the queen's cupbearer. It was his duty to taste everything before giving it to the queen. Someone must have been trying to kill Angelina."

"Will he die?"

"He's probably already dead."

"Already d—?"

"And he was one of us," Kate added solemnly. "He was a thirteen-year-old."

Before Avery had time to process this news, a heavy hand grabbed her by the shoulder and lifted her airborne. When her feet hit the ground, she whipped around to see the old woman standing behind her, a scowl etching her face.

"I had nothing to do with this!" Avery said. "I would never harm the queen!"

The old woman put a crooked finger to her lips and then whispered, "Come with me." Avery threw a helpless look at Kate on her way out the door, but Kate did not follow.

"We 'ave a problem," the woman said once they were alone in the stairwell.

"I can explain," Avery said, her mind racing to the note in the queen's dress. She did not want to be linked to the poison in any way.

"Don't talk for once; just listen. The king has demanded organ music as a distraction, and none of us play. Angelina fired our chief musician months ago."

"I play!" Avery said.

"I know. Why do you think I'm 'ere?"

Avery wanted to know how the old woman knew she played the organ, but now was not the time. The king was losing control of his banquet, and an angry king was a threat to everyone.

"Can I trust you to do as I say?" the old woman continued.

Avery nodded.

"Fine. Follow me."

They walked for many minutes, winding around the stairwell until they came to a thick door with an *X* where the old woman again put her finger to her lips. "We can't speak once the door 'ere is opened."

Avery nodded.

"The pipes from the organ will hide you. Whatever you do, stay 'idden, understand?"

Avery didn't respond.

"Do you understand?" the woman pressed.

"I will play the organ for you under one condition: you will tell me where my father and my brother are and how they are doing. Do we have an agreement?"

Avery stuck out her hand the way she saw her father do when making agreements in his shop. Of course, it rarely worked and people hardly remembered to pay their bills.

"Let's see how well you play first."

The woman pushed the door open and shoved Avery onto a gallery, following closely.

Step by nervous step, Avery walked onto a balcony that overlooked the wedding party, and a host of butterflies took flight in her stomach. She loved playing, but she had only ever played for church and family. She had never played for royalty. What would please a frantic king and a threatened queen?

Avery looked back at the door, and the old woman pointed to the bench.

"Sit," she mouthed.

The organ was far bigger and more magnificent than hers at home. She poised her fingers above the keys.

For better or for worse, this was her moment.

chapter 22

The Breakthrough

The pure and perfect sound that rose from the organ surprised even Avery as her fingers traveled up and down the keys, playing a favorite childhood tune her mother had used to calm her fears and lull her to sleep.

She wondered if she should have chosen something familiar to the guests—more festive perhaps—for the entire room below suddenly grew uncomfortably quiet.

What if the king doesn't like my music and demands to see me?

What if the old woman is angry and refuses to tell me about my family?

The song grew loud then soft then louder still before ending on a single note.

Avery peeked over her shoulder and was surprised to see tears on the old woman's face. She motioned for Avery to play another song and then another.

Happy to comply, for those few minutes she forgot the importance of her audience, forgot what the old woman had done to her in the woods, and even forgot her uncertainty over what was to come.

Such was the power of music. Avery felt what others only heard.

When she finished playing, she stood and returned to the stairs, anxious for an answer about her father and brother, but the woman was nowhere to be found. Instead, a lanky scout stood by the door with a single message.

"She said to tell you your brother is alive. She doesn't know anything about your father."

⚬∞⚬

That night, more than a dozen girls crowded around Avery to compliment her skill and ask what other instruments she played and whether she would teach them.

Suddenly, she no longer felt useless and talentless, the odd girl out.

She was still homesick and worried to death about Henry, but it felt good to smile again and mean it. When she crawled into bed and pulled the quilt up to her chin, as usual she waited until the room was still before she quietly reached into the torn seam of her pillow to retrieve the ruby necklace.

Tonight she found nothing but feathers.

Avery dug deeper, feeling for the gold chain, the ruby flower. She shook the pillow, feathers flying, hoping to hear a rattle.

Nothing.

Avery whipped off her quilt and dropped to her knees on the cold floor, no longer caring who might be awake or watching. She felt all around by the bed and underneath.

It couldn't have just slipped out. Someone had to have taken it. But who even knew where she hid it? And did they also know it had once belonged to the queen?

Being caught with royal jewels is punishable by death.

After several more frantic minutes of searching, she crawled back into bed and did the only thing she knew to do. She squeezed her eyes shut against the sting of tears and prayed God would help her find everything she had lost.

⁓⧖⁓

The next morning, with puffy eyes and pasty face, Avery knew she needed to appear casual so that whoever took the necklace wouldn't even know she knew it was gone yet.

She wanted badly to employ Kate's help, but she wasn't ready to tell her the whole story yet—especially about what she had seen in the painting of the queen—not without more facts first. Another thought occurred to her—

What if Kate took the necklace?

Avery swatted the idea away. Despite Kate's many peculiarities, she was a friend.

Yet Avery remembered with clarity her first night in the castle when Kate had removed the necklace after she had passed out. And there was the night Kate watched her stuff the necklace into her pillow. No one else had seen it.

Avery pasted her best smile over her brittle confidence as she entered the dining hall and hoped no one would talk to her during breakfast. She sat and filled her plate when Tuck stood suddenly at his spot at the center of the table and commanded the attention of the crowd.

The whole room quieted.

"Sorry to interrupt," he said, "but I have just received some news I want to share. I know you will all be excited with me."

Tuck kept looking at Avery, making her wish she felt better than she did. She had to muster all her strength to maintain her fake smile.

"The king was so pleased with the music yesterday that before he and the queen left on their honeymoon, he commissioned the organist"—and here he mimicked the king's deep voice, "'whoever he was'—to write the theme song for the Olympiad. Of course, we all know who 'he was'!"

Tuck gestured for Avery to stand, and he began clapping. Soon the others joined in, and several called out their congratulations. Avery stood, but in a moment that should have been one of the best of her life, she had to fight to keep her eyes wide open so she wouldn't burst into tears.

❧

At a cabinet meeting later that morning, Avery was surprised to find Kendrick at the table with no sign of Tuck.

Kendrick couldn't have looked more uninterested as Avery took a seat beside him.

He stifled yawns while she repressed tears.

We make a sad pair.

Today, at least, she was thankful he hated small talk. Kendrick kept his gaze straight ahead, and that was fine with her. Though, the more she thought about it, Kendrick never really looked at her. In fact, he never really looked at anyone.

The silence lay as thick as a blanket as they sat there for five minutes, then ten, and that stretched to twenty.

"Ridiculous," Kendrick said finally under his breath.

"It's what we agreed to do," Avery said in the same tone Kendrick had used with her at their first meeting.

Kendrick smiled, and Avery smiled, too.

They returned to their silence.

So much for trying to break the ice. Avery wished there was something she could say. She knew what it was like to feel isolated. They had at least that much in common.

"You never know what burdens people are carrying," Avery's mother had always told her. *"Be nice to everyone."*

"Did you know we arrived here the same day?" she asked, wondering if he had struggled the way she had. Maybe he'd left a family member behind. Maybe he, too, carried regrets.

"Yeah, so?"

Avery needed something to keep her mind off of the missing necklace. She had lost too much sleep the night before trying to consider ways she might recover it or at least explain how she got it in the event she was questioned. No easy apology would spare her the gallows.

She would avoid an untimely death and find her necklace by whatever means necessary.

She stood. "I want to show you something."

He stiffened. "Show me what?"

"Don't come if you don't want to," she said casually, "but it may be the best place in the entire castle." She moved toward the door and was relieved to hear Kendrick's chair scrape the floor.

She led him down the hall to the stairs and then up to a landing where Avery pressed her ear against a door *without* a giant red *X*. When she pushed it open, she turned to watch Kendrick's face as he carefully stepped inside.

chapter 23

A Critical Development

Kendrick looked shocked then pleased.

With the help of her mother's stories, Avery had discovered the library fit for a castle.

Here was the room that had inspired her father to build the library in the tree house. Its floor-to-ceiling shelves contained a vast array of leather-bound, golden-clasped books in every imaginable size. Rolling ladders served as bridges to an entire world of undiscovered information.

Come explore! the books seemed to whisper.

And Avery knew—even if she could read one book a day for the rest of her life—she would barely make a dent in the stacks.

The scent of leather and lemons made her wish she had all the time in the world to travel volume by volume through the entire room. The only thing that would make this moment better would be to share it with someone she loved.

She looked at Kendrick.

Unfortunately, he would have to do.

Avery pointed to the ceiling, which had been painted a most realistic dark blue with golden stars and a huge moon like the one she had seen from the raft on her way to the castle. How strange!

Light unmistakably shone through the moon, and Avery felt a breeze on her face.

But she missed *her* moon and *her* stars, the ones that had kept her company during many nights in the woods. She stood there bright-eyed and thunderstruck, waiting for Kendrick to ask the obvious questions:

Are we allowed in here?

How did you know this was here?

Should we tell Tuck?

But instead, Kendrick began a slow but deliberate climb up one of the ladders and, with a gentleness that surprised Avery, took a book from the shelf and tenderly opened it. Glancing down at her, he nodded and smiled, and she realized that was as close to a thank-you as she was likely to ever get from him. He was an odd boy, but to his defense, he had selected a book by Alfred, Lord Tennyson, the great poet laureate, and she was impressed.

> *The splendour falls on castle walls*
> *And snowy summits old in story:*
> *The long light shakes across the lakes,*
> *And the wild cataract leaps in glory.*
> *Blow, bugle, blow, set the wild echoes flying,*
> *Blow, bugle; answer, echoes, dying, dying, dying.*

Avery found her own place among the shelves and tugged a few glittering stories and dusty history books from the stacks, situated herself on the floor, and began to read, looking for information about Queen Elizabeth and her secrets.

Her only concern became having enough time to read everything she wanted.

One of the books she discovered was a Bible. She turned its onionskin pages carefully, letting the words wash over her soul like cool water on a blistering day. As she scanned, the pages seemed to come alive to her as no other book had the power to do.

Hours later—or so it seemed—Avery looked up to find Kendrick standing over her. He still didn't look her in the eye, but he appeared happier, more relaxed.

A new, unspoken bond seemed to form between them.

He held out a hand to her, whispering, "We should go."

She accepted his help, tucking the Bible under her arm as well as a copy of *Great Expectations* and *Gulliver's Travels* to borrow and return.

"Books are made for lending," her mother had always said.

Avery decided she would accept Kate's offer to attend chapel services with the other thirteen-year-olds. Reading the Bible made her hungry to know more.

As she climbed the stone stairway behind Kendrick, she was grateful she had found another friend.

⁓⊗⁓

Avery skipped supper so she could begin drawing a map of the castle.

Returning to her mattress, she was surprised to find a large, thick parchment rolled and tied with a ribbon and resting on her pillow.

She untied it and shook it open.

It was the painting of Queen Elizabeth she had discovered in storage.

But why? Who had given the painting to her?

And then her gaze came to rest on the ruby necklace. It was circled with a message.

Stop looking for it or your whole family is in danger.

Looking both ways, she lifted her mattress just enough to slide the painting underneath. She would think about how to handle this message later. For now, she had something else to do.

Relying on her day-to-day experiences and memories of the afternoon she and Kate had spent exploring, she began sketching a floor plan, noting in block letters the rooms she knew and adding a question mark for those she didn't.

The more she drew, the more she realized how accurate her mother's stories and songs about the castle had been. Avery had no doubt about her mother spending time in the castle, but when and why remained mysteries to her.

And why didn't she ever tell me?

How to get to the tunnels in the castle's underbelly remained another mystery, one she was bent on solving. If she found an entrance to the tunnels, she and the other kids would have a way of escape if they needed one. And with the unpredictability of the castle, it was likely they would need one. If the king died, escape from Angelina might be essential.

None of the doors she had tried on the lower level had yet led to anything helpful.

She was also eager to discover in which rooms Angelina spent most of her time.

Avery had meant every word in the note she had pinned in Angelina's wedding dress: *You have secrets I will uncover if you do not let us go.*

"Now I need to find what they are."

The queen's smile when she read the note confirmed everything Avery suspected about her. She was growing more confident by the day that Angelina was responsible for their confinement. Now she had to prove it, understand the reason behind it, and do something about it before the king died and left his evil wife to rule the castle.

Avery scooped up her map and tucked it in the pages of one of her library books. She had one last task to accomplish before everyone else got back from supper.

Taking the copy of *Gulliver's Travels* from the library, she wrapped it with the cloth the way she had seen her father wrap packages in his shop and carried it with her out into the hall.

She had no time to lose.

chapter 24

The Visit

Despite the warning on the painting, Avery wanted to find her necklace more than she craved her next breath. She didn't care about Ilsa's empty threats—which she suspected they were—she wanted her mother's necklace back. And she had every reason to suspect Ilsa took it.

And if Ilsa took the necklace, Kate did not. Avery desperately hoped Kate had nothing to do with the missing jewelry.

The weight of the necklace around her neck had been a constant reminder that she belonged to someone. Without it, she felt alone.

She rushed to Ilsa's room and was pleased to see only one girl inside.

"Excuse me," she said.

The girl looked up from where she appeared to be writing a letter.

"I'm wondering if you would deliver this book to Kendrick in exchange for a square of chocolate."

The girl agreed, and once she was gone, Avery snapped into action.

She examined every inch of Ilsa's space.

She shook the pillow.

She pulled the quilt off Ilsa's bed.

She felt under the mattress and discovered a nicely carved rosewood box. Hope rose and then fell when she saw that the necklace wasn't inside. She found something else inside: a stack of formal drawings, edges curling with age.

Conflicted between respecting Ilsa's property and dying of curiosity, she yielded and flipped through them.

The first showed Ilsa and a group Avery assumed was her family, because Ilsa's twin brother was there. Edward, as she learned was his name, was rumored to be the best scout and in charge of tracking the king.

The next drawing was of a small stone house.

Avery was about to replace the pages when she caught sight of one of Ilsa in the plain white dress of a country bride and a daisy chain crown—a smile stretching the width of her sun-kissed face. She looked happy.

A new look for her.

Next to her stood a beaming young man Avery could only assume was the groom. She looked closer. *Tuck?*

She held the drawing closer and tilted it toward the light.

Surely her eyes were deceiving her.

The picture showed Tuck and Ilsa, arm in arm!

No wonder Ilsa was so possessive of Tuck. If she was betrothed to him, she had every right to be jealous. But why keep their relationship a secret?

Her heart sank.

The next morning while many of the girls still slept, Avery stole away to the tiny chapel.

Light streamed through the stained-glass windows and reflected off the gold-gilded walls, almost as if the room itself knew it was time to worship. The high-back pews were filled with twenty or so kids who appeared happy to be there and pleased that she had joined them.

Avery spotted Kate near the front and hurried to sit beside her. The mousy boy with tousled hair and freckles—the one who had given Kate his hard-won grate for the wedding—shuffled to the pulpit and smiled. "Welcome," he said.

"We voted him in as chaplain at our last service," Kate whispered. "We meet here every Sunday."

Avery wondered how many services they had shared.

The chaplain led them in singing:

Praise God from whom all blessings flow!
Praise Him, all creatures here below!
Praise Him above, ye heav'nly host!
Praise Father, Son, and Holy Ghost. Amen.

He then opened his Bible and began to speak.

His voice was as high-pitched as Kate's and quavered, yet he seemed wiser than his years or scrawny frame suggested.

"In 1 Corinthians 10:31," he began, "it says, 'Whether

therefore ye eat, or drink, or whatsoever ye do, do all to the glory of God.' It is our duty as Christians to honor Him. So whether we are scrubbing floors or wearing a crown, we are equal before Him in our mission and duty. The good news is that each of us has the ability to accomplish this task."

"What did you think?" Kate asked when the service drew to a close.

"I think this chapel is a great place for self-reflection."

Kate laughed. "Silly Avery. We don't worship to reflect on ourselves. We worship to reflect on God."

⚜

The mood in the castle shifted.

Lunch became a quiet, gloomy event. Whether it was because the wedding was past and the kids no longer had anything to look forward to or because of something else entirely, Avery didn't know, but the atmosphere was toxic. Gone were the excited voices and the random laughter. Gone were the bartering and bargaining. Gone were the intense games of chess that kept kids up until the wee hours.

In place of their enthusiasm was a somber awareness that they were prisoners and that winter was coming. Avery had a powerful urge to throw open the windows and allow the sunshine and cool air to rush in and do their healing work—but she knew better.

She was feeling the heaviness, too.

After her morning council meeting, she excused herself to the kitchen, as she often did, where she went deep into the pantry and stopped at the grate over the king's office. Cranking open the slats, she looked down to see Angelina deep in conversation with a half circle of adults who were taking careful notes.

The king was nowhere to be found.

"For the ceremonial procession, I want horses—hundreds of them—and enough flower petals for seven hundred guests. I want music and soldiers and a new crown. I don't want to wear the crown of my sister."

Sister? Why did she say "sister"?

"Nothing must stop my coronation!" Angelina continued. "I must be crowned in front of everyone so it is official. I will not be robbed of my legitimate claim to the crown. Do you all understand?"

The half circle grunted their support, and the meeting concluded.

Everyone, including Angelina, left the room.

Avery waited. She knew what would happen next—

A moment later the door opened again and a scout scurried in, removed a stack of papers from the desk, and replaced it with a stack of mail.

Avery smiled.

The castle was a well-oiled machine being run, at least in part, by the willpower of thirteen-year-olds.

⌘

Avery waited until the kids were on the way to their rooms for afternoon rest.

She tapped Tuck on the shoulder. "May I talk to you alone?"

Avery hated the way her heart raced whenever she spoke to him, especially after she had seen the drawing of him and Ilsa. If Tuck was spoken for—even if their courtship had been forged in childhood—she must not fan the flame of her feelings for him.

Tuck motioned for her to follow him to the sitting room just off of the dining room.

They stood in the center of the room.

"We need a new system," Avery began as she paced and gestured. "Everyone here needs something, and everyone here can offer something. When people feel useless, they become unproductive, and when that happens, chaos ensues."

Tuck smiled. "You've really thought this through, haven't you?"

"Another thing. We should pay the kids for their work. Otherwise, what's the point of all of this? A workman is worthy of his hire, right? It says so in the Bible."

Tuck laughed, and Avery stopped pacing.

"Sorry," Tuck said, holding up his hands and collapsing into a chair. "No problem with anything you've said, except we don't have any money. And what would we be able to do with money anyway? But I admire your passion."

"We don't need money. We have something better. Follow me."

Tuck followed her to the storage room and the collection she and Kate had discovered. She watched carefully to see how he reacted to seeing the rich mahogany furniture, glass bottles, and crates of knickknacks—a lifetime of treasures in one room.

"Incredible," he said. "How did you know this was in here?"

"I was looking for grates," she said. "But that doesn't matter.

What matters is what I'd like to do with this."

Tuck listened for nearly an hour, adding his own thoughts during those rare instances when Avery stopped to take a breath.

"Thanks for listening," Avery said.

Tuck smiled. "I'll listen to you anytime." Then he winked, and there went her pulse again, racing without her permission.

"So I can start right away?" Avery pressed.

Tuck nodded.

She needed to ask him about the connection between Angelina and Elizabeth.

She also needed to muster the courage to ask him about Ilsa—and soon.

But first she would need to find a logical reason to do so.

chapter 25

The Envelope

As afternoon gave way to evening and the kids began retiring, Avery rolled up her sleeves and, together with Kate, made a hundred trips between the storage room and the great room where the kids had held their chess tournaments on happier days.

She was determined to bring enthusiasm back to the space.

The two girls lugged boxes of treasures and heavy pieces of furniture, propped beautiful paintings against the walls, and hung jewelry from brass candle stands. They filled tables with the treasures of the castle and collected crates full of glass marbles.

Avery set up the room to look as much like her father's shop as she could remember, and it made her happier than she thought possible.

When she and Kate were done, they stared wide-eyed at the transformation. The room had become a chamber worthy of a castle.

When the kids saw it the next morning after breakfast—at Tuck's insistence—Avery watched their expressions transform from weariness to shock.

Whispers rose like the smoke from a thousand chimneys.

Avery waited until they had all assembled in a giant circle

before she called for their attention. She realized something as she looked out over the crowd of faces—

Weeks of living in hiding without sun or fresh air had taken their toll.

The kids look pale and tired.

She knew that they, like she, would love to feel the wind on their faces and the grass beneath their feet. Autumn would soon give way to winter if Avery had calculated the days correctly, and she hoped they would all be long gone before the first real snow, but she had no reason to believe that would happen.

Her hope, like theirs she guessed, had been replaced by grim resignation.

She clapped until a hush fell over the crowd, and when she caught sight of Tuck smiling at her from the back, she pressed forward with renewed confidence.

"I was reminded Sunday that whether we are scrubbing floors or wearing a crown, we are responsible to do our work well before God."

No one looked impressed.

"I also believe we should be rewarded for the work we do."

That got their attention.

"So beginning today, you will be paid for your effort."

The kids began to whisper.

How long had it been—if ever—since these kids had been paid for their labor? Many had lived off the village scraps before being brought to the castle. For some, their sole job had been survival. Payment had been going to sleep with a full stomach.

Kate and her circle of seamstresses appeared suddenly, carrying baskets of tiny velvet pouches they had sewn, and they distributed one to each teen. The kids opened them and dumped the contents into their hands.

"Marbles?" someone asked, clearly irritated.

"What are we supposed to do with these?" another called out. "Is this some sort of joke?"

The room erupted.

As quickly as Avery had climbed in their favor, she fell.

Avery tried to call over the rumble to no avail. She picked up the bucket Tuck had used on the night he was made king and turned it over. She stood on it and called over the noise.

"Give me your attention!" she bellowed.

The room stilled.

"What is money but an idea? Money is only copper or paper used to trade for desired goods. What you hold in your hand is just like money. Look around. Kate and I have set up shop. We can pay you in treasures, and there are plenty more where these came from. The scouts have agreed to watch for items downstairs as well. You can exchange marbles for anything you see in this room. All prices can be bartered."

"And it's ours to keep?"

"For as long as we're here."

She explained how many marbles the kids would earn for each task and how much each item cost, but the kids had stopped listening and were already walking around admiring the merchandise.

A light had returned in the darkness.

That night—exhausted after bartering all day over every imaginable trinket—Avery was excited to see how much better the bunk room looked. Rich furniture had replaced the drab wardrobes, and elaborate pillows and colorful blankets decorated the beds. Girls sat comparing purchases and making trades, and it reminded Avery of the days she used to spend at Godfrey's.

For years she had watched her father order items, display them in his smudge-free picture window, barter with his customers, and eventually wrap the items and send them off. He had always taken pride in his work, even when Avery had been embarrassed that he was *only a shopkeeper*.

Avery liked to imagine he would have been pleased with what she had done today.

Though, no doubt, he would have offered suggestions for improvement.

And, no doubt, she would have been agitated that he was right.

She took off her slippers and changed into her nightgown. She hadn't gotten much sleep the night before and wanted desperately to stretch out on her mattress and close her eyes. She pulled back the blanket and crawled inside.

As she did every night, she checked her pillow on the remote chance that whoever had stolen her necklace might have returned it.

There was no necklace.

But something else.

In the spot beneath her pillow was a carefully folded parcel. It looked like any of the countless letters Kendrick sorted each afternoon in the dining room. Sometimes he opened them using the flame of a candle to soften the seal so he could reseal the letter before delivering it to the king. It was always folded in thirds like this one.

Avery turned it over. *Red wax.*

Kendrick always uses red wax when sealing letters he has written on behalf of the king.

She was about to lift the letter to get a better look at the center of the seal, where an emblem had been stamped, when a voice behind her said—

"Bed already? You're usually a night owl."

Avery dropped her pillow and turned to Kate. "I'm just tired."

"Long day," Kate said, smiling. "Everyone seemed happy. Today was a win for you."

Avery nodded. "A win for *us*. We start again tomorrow!"

She lay back on her pillow wanting nothing more than to tear open the letter. *Kate enjoys a surprise as much as I do.* But something compelled her to keep the letter a secret. And so she avoided the subject.

"Do you think we'll be able to maintain the shop?" Avery asked.

"With Angelina's shifting tastes, we should be in business a long time."

At least an hour passed before the room finally quieted and the fire in the hearth died away.

Avery thought she might explode if she had to wait another minute. When she was sure she was the only one awake, she slipped out of bed, letter in hand, and tiptoed barefoot in the dark, feeling her way down the hall to the washroom with the copper tub.

Thankful to find a lone match in the box, she lit a candle and sat on the floor, using Kendrick's technique to soften the seal and open the parcel.

She unfolded the page and smoothed it against her lap, finding one neat, careful line of penmanship:

I could but stay one hundred years if I knew you would stay here, too.

It was unsigned.
Who could it be from?

chapter 26

Holiday Hope

On Christmas Day the king and queen held an extravagant holiday banquet in the hall where they were married.

All the kids—even those who didn't normally attend—participated in a chapel service upstairs. Packed like sardines in the tiny space, they lit tall white candles and sang half a dozen songs, including:

Sleep, my child, and peace attend thee,
All through the night.
Guardian angels God will send thee,
All through the night.
Soft the drowsy hours are creeping,
Hill and vale in slumber steeping,
I my loving vigil keeping
All through the night.

Avery expected the chaplain to read from Luke 2 about the birth of Christ, but the boy instead referred to Ephesians 4.

"We are commanded to be kind, tender of heart, and forgiving toward each other. These are the gifts we can give each other throughout the year when the holiday has passed. We are instructed to forgive in the same way Jesus Christ has forgiven us—not halfheartedly or self-righteously, but entirely. Forgiveness is the greatest gift God has given us. We forgive because He forgave."

Avery could see Ilsa from where she sat. She couldn't imagine ever being able to forgive her. Not only had she been unkind from day one, but she knew something about the missing necklace, and she had laid claim to Tuck's heart.

Avery was certain of it.

⋘⋙

The kids who were not needed to help with the banquet downstairs spent the afternoon enjoying arm wrestling and chess matches while the kitchen workers brought in silver trays loaded with scraps from the banquet. Only on holidays were the doors to the castle open and the public welcome inside. Rumor had it three hundred people were dining with the king and queen, so they were oblivious to any extra noise the kids were making.

It was a good thing, because the kids were in a festive mood.

Tuck gathered a group in an empty gallery that had a black-and-white checkered floor, chose up sides, and assigned each person a role as a chess piece: two kings, two queens, four rooks, four bishops, four knights, and sixteen pawns.

Then they began a game of human chess.

Tuck was the king of his team with Avery as queen, while Kendrick led the other with Kate as his queen. The kings called out strategic moves and taunted each other when pieces were lost. Friendly insults were tossed back and forth, and strategizing was kicked into high gear.

Several booted pawns stalked off to their bunk rooms.

"If you are my queen, we should make it official, don't you think?" Tuck asked Avery in the heat of the game.

Avery looked at him, unsure what he meant.

"Hold out your hand," he said.

Confused, Avery did as she was told.

Tuck dropped something small and shiny into it.

Avery looked down to see a small gold ring, shaped like a crown, with small pointed spikes.

Is this just for the length of the game?

"Merry Christmas!" he said, before making fun of Kendrick for a lousy decision involving his bishop.

"You, too?" she asked as an afterthought. She slipped the ring onto her right hand and suppressed a smile, telling herself, *It's Christmas. He is just being kind. He is my friend, after all. Friends give each other Christmas gifts.*

Avery couldn't remember when she had had so much fun, and it didn't escape her that Tuck kept smiling at her. Kendrick watched her, too.

Then the old woman appeared. "Avery, you 'ave been summoned to the organ."

She wasn't halfway to the door before Ilsa replaced her as queen in the chess game.

And another good thing came screeching to a halt.

As Avery followed the old woman through the stairwell, she whispered, "Where is Henry? Can I at least send him a holiday message? I know you know where he is."

The old woman looked agitated, but she didn't deny it.

Avery stopped walking. "I won't play another note until you help me."

The old woman laughed. "I could 'ave you exiled or even killed this afternoon for any number of crimes. Rumor is, you were found with the queen's ruby necklace. You are in no position to barter with me."

Avery's stomach tightened and a lump formed in her throat.

"Fine, but you still need an organist. And Angelina doesn't take no for an answer. If you send me to the Forbidden City, you won't have anyone to play when she demands it, so your head will be on the chopping block, too."

Avery and the old woman stood nose to nose in cold silence.

"What message do you want me to deliver?"

"Tell Henry I love him and I am coming for him. And tell him I am so sorry."

"Fine," said the old woman. "Only if the king is pleased with how you play."

"How did you know I had the necklace?"

"You underestimate what I know."

❦

Lutes played and people laughed below as Avery sat and played every Christmas song she knew. Still, the old woman urged her to continue.

At a loss, Avery decided to play a festive song she had arranged for her parents on their last wedding anniversary. It was a simple tune her mother had sung to her every night before bed. The words began—

Avery, dear, you're the rose in my garden,
The sun in my sky, and the wind in my sails.

She had barely begun to play when a shriek rose up from the guests.

"Get the medic!" a man called out.

More poison? Another botched assassination attempt?

Avery stopped and turned to see what the old woman wanted her to do, but she had vanished. Avery heard silverware clanking, chairs scraping, and skirts whooshing. Cries rose above the crowd.

"She's passed out!"

With no one to stop her, Avery tiptoed to the edge of the balcony—which she knew was strictly forbidden—and peered down on the crowd that had gathered around Angelina. Someone held her while others tried to cool her with elaborate handheld fans. Even unconscious, Angelina was beautiful.

"Who played that song?" someone called.

Shouts tore through the crowd.

"That song belonged to Queen Elizabeth!"

"Whoever played it should be punished!"

"To the organ!"

Avery knew it would be a matter of seconds before adults rushed the stairs and scoured the gallery looking for the guilty musician, so she raced to safety. Into the stairwell and up the steps—two at a time—she went, the train of her dress whipping behind her. She was thankful for her gift of speed and only stopped to catch her breath when she was safely hidden in the children's quarters.

⚬✄⚬

Later that night in the great room, Avery watched a pair of boys trade jousts with wooden swords, wondering what consequences she might face if she was found out. The old woman certainly wouldn't deliver the message to Henry now.

She imagined the old woman whisking her to some terrible place.

The Forbidden City? The chopping block?

Avery had learned that the Forbidden City sat a mile and a half offshore and was home to the most offensive criminals or traitors as determined by the king or queen. Because of its extreme isolation from the outside world—it could only be accessed by boat—people who were sent to the Forbidden City were rarely, if ever, heard from again.

Avery wondered if thirteen-year-olds ever constituted offensive criminals or traitors.

"She's fine," Kate said, sitting down next to Avery on a plush chair in the great room. "Scouts have been tracking Angelina all afternoon and have sent word that she recovered just fine in the care of her medic. She never passes on an opportunity for drama. You should be able to appreciate that."

"How could I possibly have known?" she asked Kate for the hundredth time.

Kate had explained that the original lyrics to the fateful song had been:

Elizabeth, you're the rose in my garden,
The sun in my sky, and the wind in my sails.

"You didn't know," Kate assured her, "so don't worry about it."

"How do *you* know that song, Kate?"

Kate shrugged. "I know a lot of castle history."

I've noticed.

Kate was growing more mysterious every day. Only a thirteen-year-old seamstress, yet she had an answer to Avery's every question. Sometimes Avery created difficult questions just to stump her, but it never worked.

Quietly Avery asked, "If you could return to your old life, would you do it?"

Kate looked suddenly uncomfortable.

She was spared an answer because a boy dressed entirely in black paraded out onto a makeshift stage in the center of the great room. "May I have your attention?" he called.

The room grew quiet as everyone turned to see what he wanted.

"Tonight you will observe the royal wedding as it was meant

to be! Please, gather around!"

Curious kids from all corners of the room came to sit around the stage.

Kate grabbed Avery's arm and tugged her to the circle.

"I love plays!" she said. "Come on!"

From offstage, a group of kids began to sing in exaggerated high-pitched voices, and a girl appeared in an oversize ivory dress, her red hair piled ridiculously high above her head, with a cat—presumably a fake one—resting on top.

"Can you do nothing right?" the girl in the wedding dress asked the singers in a whiny voice as the audience of children laughed and clapped. She took her place on the stage, and a group of boys made exaggerated trumpet sounds with their hands cupped over their mouths.

A boy wearing a heavy purple cloak and a large gold crown entered the room and marched to the stage. Wanting to resemble the king's large stomach, the boy had stuffed straw under his shirt, but to his dismay, he was losing straw by the handful the longer he stood there. With one hand he held his cloak in place, and with the other hand he desperately held the bottom of his shirt while the children roared with laughter.

"I do take thee to be my wedded wife," he said as straw spilled out of his shirt, "for worse or for even worse." More straw spilled around him.

Avery couldn't remember a time she had laughed so hard.

"Must I do everything myself?" the girl playing Angelina asked, bending over and picking up the handfuls of straw and handing them to the boy, who reached out his hand and lost his grip on the cloak just as the cat from "Angelina's" hair came tumbling down.

The play went long into the night until a child wearing a funny pointy hat proclaimed the two married, and the room erupted in applause.

∞

Avery wondered what her father and Henry were doing to celebrate the day. She had always complained about what little she received from her parents on Christmas, but now she would trade everything—the dresses, the food, the library—to have her old life back, even for one day.

She could still hear her father's voice in her head, reading the final line of the Christmas story from the pages of his well-read Bible—

" *'But Mary kept all these things, and pondered them in her heart.'* "

Avery was learning what it was to *ponder* things.

She was thinking about returning to her room to work on her floor plans of the castle when she caught Kendrick watching her from across the room. He stood by the table of food trays, but he was definitely watching her—something that made no sense. Despite working with him and Tuck and visiting the library with him occasionally, Avery felt she knew little about him. He still refused to look her in the eye when they talked.

But now he mouthed something she couldn't distinguish and nodded before leaving the room with a pack of boys. Avery noticed a wrapped package at the table where he had stood. Had he meant to leave it behind? If not, she could grab the package and follow after him so he wouldn't wonder later where he had left it.

There was only one way to find out.

She went to it. On a tiny square of parchment atop it, she found her name in careful script. She untied a golden thread and removed the cloth to find a copy of *A Tale of Two Cities*. Like the book she had sent Kendrick, it had gold leaf pages and a leather cover clamped with a brass clasp.

He was returning the favor. She had sent him *Gulliver's Travels*, and now he was sending her *A Tale of Two Cities*. Maybe their friendship would work after all. A relationship built on books wasn't half bad.

Kate reappeared and grabbed her arm. "Quickly, come with me!"

Avery followed Kate into the hallway to the stairwell where they climbed the steps two at a time to a room at the highest point in the castle. Kate ran to the window and pulled the heavy drapes aside, the thin moonlight glowing on her pale, pretty face. Whatever suspicions Avery had of her were gone in a heartbeat.

"Aren't you going to come see?" Kate asked.

Avery nodded but remained frozen where she stood. Was this the moment she had been waiting for? Would she finally be able to recognize something from the window? Had Kate discovered her father's whaleboat in the harbor? Christmas would be the perfect day to feel some sort of hope about home.

Finally she forced herself to take slow, deliberate steps to where she could look out over the village, radiant with the Christmas spirit.

Tears welled up in her eyes in anticipation.

chapter 27

Missing!

Avery scanned the marina, trying to distinguish one boat from the other.

The streets were crowded with the clatter of carts and the clopping of horses on timeworn cobblestones. Fat flakes dusted the roads below like sugar on fried dough.

Tiny wisps of smoke rose from the chimneys, and vessels forged their way through the frigid Salt Sea. How long, she wondered, before the water would be frozen and the crafts would be stowed for the winter?

She pressed her forehead against the window, feeling the cold against her skin.

The inky sky made it impossible to see clearly. "Kate, I don't see anything I recognize."

"Just keep looking, Avery."

She narrowed her eyes and looked again.

Suddenly, the sky exploded with red, blue, and green fireworks, bursts that rocked the village and showered trails of glitter to celebrate Christmas.

"Angelina loves fireworks," Kate said with a sigh, "so the king ordered these for her. Maybe he does love her after all. Isn't it wonderful? Maybe their marriage *will* be good for the castle!"

Avery knew with a sinking feeling that this was all Kate had in mind.

No whaleboat. No promise of my father coming to my rescue. No word of Henry's safety.

"Aren't they beautiful?" Kate asked, but Avery couldn't speak.

He is doing fine. He probably spent Christmas with friends in the village.

But Avery knew she should stop being so naive.

No help is on the way. No one is coming to rescue you.

The choice was simple, and the sooner she acknowledged it the better: *Run to save your family or stay to save your life.*

With nothing to lose, it was time to risk everything.

❧

Late the next afternoon, sitting at the long wooden table, Avery spread a stack of blank pages before her in the otherwise empty dining room and listed what she knew about both the past and current queens, putting a star beside every fact she had learned from Kate.

Seeing it in writing, she realized Kate had been the source of nearly all her information.

Impossible that she would know all of this information just by paying attention.

"Sorry to interrupt," Tuck said, dropping into a chair beside her. "Do you have a moment?"

How could she refuse? She twisted the gold ring on her right hand nervously. And anyway, she didn't want to make a show of gathering her papers, so she shrugged and smiled.

"The king has commissioned you to write the theme song for the Olympiad—"

"So you announced. Is that still the plan, considering the fact that I almost killed Angelina the last time I was at the organ?"

Tuck threw his head back and laughed. "You didn't *almost kill her*. Not to mention, the king has no idea who you are. All he knows is that he loves your music. He didn't even order an investigation after the incident with Angelina. I just wanted to make sure you were planning something very special. Make it the best work you've ever done."

Avery assured Tuck she was taking it seriously, and he quickly left, but the conversation got her thinking. Her nagging suspicion was looking more likely all the time. Was it possible that the king was not the driving force behind the kids' captivity? Could it be Angelina alone? She had responded to the note in her dress without even a whiff of alarm—in fact, she had smiled! And she didn't share the note with the king. If he were in on the secret, she would have shared the message with him.

Her mind continued to travel over recent events.

If the king and Angelina were united, shouldn't he have been equally enraged about Queen Elizabeth's song being played at the Christmas banquet? But he ordered no investigation, let alone any word of potential punishment. What if he still cherished Queen Elizabeth as Avery suspected he did?

Avery looked at her notes. And a deep-seated certainty took root within her.

My mother knew about this castle because she knew Queen Elizabeth. How else could she have Queen Elizabeth's necklace in her possession? And if Queen Elizabeth is sister to Queen Angelina, my mother likely knew her, too. I need to find my father so he can help me put the pieces together and save the thirteen-year-olds.

Or else I need to find my mother.

Avery felt confident the king still harbored feelings for his first wife. He and Angelina clearly had separate agendas—Avery only needed to figure out what they were before something terrible happened to the king and Angelina was left in charge.

⚬≪∞≫⚬

That night, Kate woke Avery from a sound sleep—*again*—but judging from Kate's demeanor, this was no adventure. Something was wrong.

"What now?" Avery whispered.

"Just put this on and come with me." Kate handed her the black dress she had worn the day before and led her all the way to the dining room.

There Ilsa sat between Tuck and Kendrick, sobbing, the sound raw and horrible.

Kate finally explained. "We believe her brother was discovered."

"Discovered? By whom?"

"We don't know," Tuck said. "He disappeared while scouting during the king's Christmas banquet. Normally he tracks the king, but tonight he was tracking Angelina."

"He's the best you have," Avery said. "Maybe he's onto

something and needs more time."

Tuck shook his head.

It was Kendrick who spoke next. "Angelina went to bed hours ago. No one has seen or heard from him since the fireworks. He never came to bed. It's not like him. We can only assume the worst."

"The Forbidden City?" Avery whispered, but the others just looked away as Ilsa's wailing reached a nonhuman pitch. Avery raised her voice. "So what do we do now?"

"We need a plan," Tuck said. "We don't know what he'll tell whoever has him. Angelina's staff is very good at making people talk. We could all be in danger."

"Edward," Ilsa said miserably, liquid leaking from her eyes and nose. "His name is Edward, Tuck. I know all you care about is your own safety, but Edward is the last person I have on this earth, especially since you abandoned our family."

Tuck reddened, and Avery's thoughts raced to the drawing in the wooden box.

She tucked her hand with the crown ring behind her back.

"You've known Edward all your life, and you haven't even mentioned his name tonight," Ilsa said. "I don't care what he means to the rest of you. He's my brother, and I need him. Our first strategy should not be protecting the rest of us—it should be getting him back."

These words brought another round of tears.

"You're right," Avery said. "We will find a way." She pulled out a chair and sat across from Ilsa. "Tuck, Kendrick, what do we need to do to bring Edward back?"

"You're so stupid!" Ilsa blurted, leaping from her chair and marching toward the hall.

Kate started after her, but Tuck put up a hand to stop her. "Don't go. It won't help."

Kendrick added, "We need to stay up and talk this through. Kate, do you know where we could get some coffee?"

Kate nodded, and together they disappeared.

With Kate and Kendrick out of the room, Avery said quietly, "Pardon me for asking, Tuck, but what did she mean about you abandoning her family?"

"It's a personal thing."

"Right. It's none of my busi—"

"No, no. It's just that a year ago or so, she and I were in a silly little play in our village where we played Romeo and Juliet. Somebody drew a picture of us, and she got it in her head that it was meant to be someday, you know? We've known each other our entire lives, but. . ."

Avery felt something like relief wash over her. The drawing in the rosewood box wasn't of a wedding at all—it was of a play.

"I love plays," she said brightly.

Tuck only gave her a curious look.

Soon they all sat nursing hot mugs.

"If Edward was caught by adults, he won't be back," Tuck said, "and Ilsa knows it. I'm sorry, but protecting the rest of the kids isn't disrespecting him. It's the right thing to do. It's the job we've pledged to do as a cabinet."

"We need to find a place to hide if our location is compromised," Kendrick said.

"The passageways," Avery said.

"Have you had any success locating the tunnels?" Tuck asked.

All eyes turned to Avery.

"My mother always talked about tunnels in the castle. I've never seen them, but everything else she said has proven to be true. According to her stories, this castle sits atop an intricate system of tunnels that travels various outlets within the village. If the rumors are correct, the largest tunnel snakes its way under the Salt Sea and ends within the walls of a tiny, beautiful chapel in the village where country girls get married."

She made eye contact with Tuck, and her face went crimson. This time when he smiled she didn't look away.

chapter 28

The View from the Turret

Breakfast was a somber event as news of Edward's disappearance made its way around the table. The seat where he normally sat was left empty in his honor. Questions like *What will happen to him?* and *Are we all in danger?* rose with the steam from the kids' mugs.

But no one had answers.

Ilsa didn't come to breakfast.

No chess games or marble bartering would fix this latest disappointment.

Ilsa planned a private prayer service for Edward in the chapel upstairs, but she sent a distinct message to Avery via one of the scouts that she was not invited.

By the time Avery finished her meal, all she wanted was to be alone.

"I'm going to be a few minutes late to the shop," she whispered to Kate, who indicated that wouldn't be a problem since no one was buying anything today.

Avery made her way back to the bunk room where her pages of careful notes seemed to be calling her name. But when she sat and lifted her pillow, in addition to her notes, she found another carefully folded parcel with a red wax seal. Glancing both ways to be sure no one watched, she found a candle and opened it, smoothing the page on her mattress.

You are the Salt Sea.
And I am one who loves the waves yet does not own a compass.

Those words and the ones that followed made Avery's pulse pound.

Who keeps sending these messages?

It was not until after lunch that something occurred to her. She rushed back to the bunk room and compared the handwriting in the poem to the tiny square of parchment that had been included with the copy of *A Tale of Two Cities* Kendrick had given her on Christmas Day.

Sure enough, it was identical.

Kendrick was sending the secret messages.

⚬◈◠

Late that afternoon, her mind full of queens, worries about Ilsa's brother Edward, and confusion over her strange friendship with Kendrick, Avery escaped to the library, determined to find a book about the castle itself and its mysterious tunnels. Maybe part of her hoped she would happen upon Kendrick there, too, or he would happen upon her—so she could ask him to stop sending the parcels. Kendrick was every bit a brother and nothing more.

All she knew was that she could not wait to be among the stacks.

As usual, after her climb through the stairwell, she pressed her ear against the door to be sure it was quiet inside. Satisfied, she pushed it open, then stopped in horror.

One entire wall of the library had been ransacked, the shelves swept bare, and hundreds of books lay in piles, splayed open, their pages bent like someone had marched across the tops of them. The library floor was barely visible for the books.

Against her better judgment, she stepped inside.

Someone else is searching for the secrets in this castle.

But who else would care?

And what did they find?

"Hello?" she called. "Is anyone in here?" She stepped over piles of books, doing her best to step on the rare patches of bare ground amid the sea of pages. She heard a rustle in one corner of the room and froze. "Who's there?" she asked.

"Go away," a voice whispered. "You're not welcome in here."

"I won't go until you tell me what happened to this library."

The person laughed—a high-pitched sound—and Avery saw that the woman was hidden entirely in a heavy cloak. "Stop looking for it or your whole family is in danger."

The same words that were scrawled on the painting of Queen Elizabeth beside the ruby necklace.

Only when the cloaked figure said her name did Avery turn and flee.

She wouldn't tell anyone what happened, because it would involve explaining she was somewhere she was not allowed to be.

A few days later, Avery awoke aching with homesickness and missing her brother, her mother, and her father terribly. She pulled a plum-colored dress over her head and tugged at her hair until it fell down her back in a thick, glossy braid. In her silver slippers and pearl tiara, she headed toward breakfast, only to find Tuck in the hall, a basket in his hand and a smile on his face.

"Good morning!" he said, his eyes twinkling the way they did when he was up to something.

"Good morning," Avery said, laughing at his enthusiasm.

"I thought we could have a picnic." He tapped the basket. "Someone told me New Year's Eve is your favorite day of the year."

Well, it used to be. She shook her head.

"It isn't?" he said.

Avery nodded.

"Well, which is it?"

"It is." Avery wondered why every time she talked to Tuck she managed to embarrass herself. Maybe just once she could have a conversation with him that didn't make her want to hide in a wardrobe for the rest of her life.

"Well, then, would you do me the honor of sharing a picnic?"

He held out a hand and Avery took it.

They took several flights of stairs until they arrived at a door at the top of the castle.

"Miss Avery Godfrey, do you know what this leads to?" Tuck asked, still holding her hand.

She shook her head. This was one of the few wings she had not explored. It would be good for her floor plans to see what lay on the other side.

"Open it," he said.

When she did, natural light poured in, and with it, cold air that tasted like heaven.

"It's a watch turret," Tuck said, stepping out and tugging Avery with him.

"Are we allowed? Isn't this forbidden?"

"This castle has a hundred lookouts that face the Salt Sea, but unless the castle is in trouble, this tower remains unmanned. At least, that's what Edward told me."

At the mention of his name, Avery and Tuck shifted their gazes. Edward's absence was still acutely felt among the kids. Never was a meeting held or a prayer uttered in which his name was not mentioned.

It took Avery a moment to notice a quilt spread on the floor bearing two tin plates, two mugs, and two cloth napkins.

Tuck had thought of everything.

Avery stepped to the edge of the lookout, closed her eyes against the brightness of the sun, and let the wind whip her hair. It had been too long since she had tasted the world outside. For a glorious moment she felt free.

"Thank you, Tuck."

"There's something I've been meaning to tell you," he said softly, shrugging out of his coat and slipping it over her shoulders. "It's why I brought you up here."

A horn sounded on the sea, and Avery studied a barge as it moved slowly on the horizon.

She was relieved to have a reason not to need to face Tuck. His voice sounded strangely serious.

When he laid a hand on her shoulder, she desperately scanned the shore for houses and shops she recognized.

Tuck began talking about how time changes people.

Strange.

Were those the woods where she and Henry had played? Was it possible to see them from the castle? She had certainly never seen the castle from her tree house in the woods.

Tuck talked about how it was only natural for feelings to grow over time—even ones that couldn't be explained.

Maybe I never recognized anything when I looked out the window because I needed a better angle.

Avery narrowed her eyes and carefully mapped the location, tracing a line between the woods and where her house belonged.

"What I am trying to say is that you are important to me," Tuck said.

And everything screeched to a halt.

Home. She could see her home!

At least she thought she could see her home!

And a dark plume of smoke rose from the chimney.

Avery turned around to face him, tears dotting her eyes.

"I need to go," she said, slipping out of his coat and leaving him in midsentence. She took the stairs as quickly as she could, running until her sides ached, tripping on her dress, legs moving like jelly.

"Avery!" Tuck called out. "Come back! I didn't mean to offend you."

He's home! she told herself over and over as she ran. *My father is home!*

He had probably been home all along.

And now it was time for her to go home, too. He could help her find Henry!

chapter 29

The Whisper of Home

As quickly as she could, Avery emptied her feather pillow, the feathers falling in clumps onto her mattress. She took the Bible she had come to love, her notes and map, and a couple of candles and matchsticks, stashing everything in her now-empty pillowcase.

Henry, hang on. I am coming home. If you're not there yet, Father will know what to do.

She removed the red ribbon from her wrist and the pearl tiara from atop her head and left them on Kate's pillow, hoping to send the message that she had left of her own will. She didn't want Kate to know she was leaving before she was gone, but she didn't want Kate to worry, either. The kids would assume she had been sent, like Edward, to the Forbidden City.

Finally, her heart thrumming in her ears, she changed into the black velvet dress with the long sleeves, hoping it would not only keep her warm, but also make her look older. Somehow she had to elude the relentless guards. Rumor had it they were the ones who had caught Edward and sent him away.

It was a risk she was willing to take.

Today was a holiday. If ever she could slip past them, it would be now.

Avery glanced around the bunk room. She hated leaving without her mother's necklace—especially after all her repeated instructions never to lose it—but what choice did she have?

From the kitchen she retrieved three apples, a crusty loaf of bread, a small pot of butter, and a few chunks of chocolate, which she hoped would hold her until she got home.

Home. The word made her smile.

Bulging pillowcase under her arm, she moved quickly to the room where she and Kate organized the queen's castoffs for the kids' shop. She wandered among the boxes until she found a dark cape with a heavy hood, along with several tiny pots that held powders, creams, and lip stains.

Using a gilded hand mirror from the to-be-bartered pile, she applied to her face crimson lips, pink cheeks, and black eyelashes. She twisted her braid into a tight bun and tucked the loose hairs up with hairpins, the way she had seen Kate do it. She slid a thick gold ring onto the ring finger of her left hand, looped two strands of pearls around her neck, and donned the cape, pulling the hood up over her face so no one would recognize her.

Already she could hear the voices of her friends outside, and it pained her not to say good-bye. She would miss Kate, Tuck, and even Kendrick, but soon the stairway would be filled with kids leaving breakfast to begin their morning tasks. The time to move was now or never.

Nodding her farewell, she raced down the stairs, face concealed and cape flying behind her, and pushed open the door that led to the Great Hall where people from the village came and went.

Since it was a holiday, the doors were unlocked and a river of people swelled in anticipation of seeing Angelina or the king. Often on holidays the royals would distribute handfuls of gold coins to the poor, so today people had come from miles around, hoping to be one of the lucky few.

Avery often wondered why the children didn't plan a holiday like this one to make a great escape. According to Kate, teenagers leaving en masse would draw attention and they would be uncovered. Additionally, they had prices on their heads as if they were outlaws. The threats in the outside world were greater than the threats of staying hidden in the castle. Not to mention, the old woman promised to bring harm to their siblings if they escaped.

Avery believed—if she got to her father safely—he would be able to help.

None of the other children had parents waiting for them.

She needed to get home quickly before the old woman could harm Henry.

Avery scooted through the crowd, the noise at a fever pitch as bodies pressed against hers to move closer to the inner entrance. She was the salmon swimming upstream.

When she tripped over a man's gnarled cane, she looked up to find a guard staring at her.

Just keep walking, she told herself, determined not to look again so he could not see her fear or her age. But out of the corner of her eye she could tell he was walking in lockstep with her.

Be calm. Act normal.

Not easy when she was trembling beneath her cape, the pillowcase pressed to her side. She would use the pillowcase as a weapon if need be.

I am wearing the queen's jewels, she thought. *I cannot get caught.*

By the time Avery reached the gate that led out of the castle and into the bright sunlight, she was gasping, her stomach knotted, eyes burning.

A hand clutched her shoulder, and her knees went weak.

She would not be stopped now, no matter if the guard was three times her size. Avery spun with a clenched fist, only to face an old woman, skinny and hunched.

"Do you have any food for the poor?" she asked, eyes glazed and wearing a peculiar, far-off expression.

Avery reached under the cloak into her pillowcase and pressed all of her food into the woman's hands. She would be home in time for supper and wouldn't need the castle's scraps. As an afterthought, she pulled a strand of beads from her neck and placed it around the woman's, which would provide her with a month of food and drink if she sold it for the right price.

The old woman grasped Avery's wrist, and for a frightful moment Avery thought she had discovered the star that would give her away.

"Bless you," the woman said, squeezing her wrist with crooked, swollen fingers. Avery hurried away, savoring her first taste of freedom without so much as a glance back at the castle.

All afternoon and into the frigid evening, Avery navigated steep declines and climbed hills that took her breath away. The air was bitter cold, and the stark sky was blanketed with winter-white stars. She wondered a hundred times how the old woman had managed to push the cart so far for so long when Avery could barely put one slippered foot in front of the other.

She would have quit but for the prospect of home and rescuing Henry.

"The road home is always longest," her mother had said on countless journeys from the shop or market.

Hours of travel once again felt like days.

By the time she reached the Salt Sea, Avery's breath came in white puffs, and she felt as if she could sleep for days. Her bones burned from the cold and her feet ached. She regretted not having taken the time to look for her boots back in the bunk room. The cloak weighed a thousand pounds on her shoulders.

She almost regretted leaving the bunk room at all.

She called out to a young man who was about to push off on a bamboo raft. He stopped with a wary scowl.

"May I ride with you to the other side?" she asked.

Skepticism filled his eyes, and Avery wondered if she were wearing her age like a badge. Orphans, according to Kate, were worth handsome bounties from the king. Avery instinctively tucked behind her the wrist marked with the star.

She flashed the thick gold ring on her left hand.

"I'll give you my wedding band. It's worth a fortune."

His eyes widened, and he reached to help her aboard.

As she sat, tucking the cape closer around her, he thrust out his hand as if expecting the ring. But Avery was tired of being swindled, of not knowing whom to trust. She narrowed her eyes at him.

"When we reach shore," she said. "You have my word."

And as the raft glided into the sea, Avery finally looked back at the castle for the first time. It looked again to her like a pyramid of gold perched on a pile of puffy clouds. Had she seen the castle from her home in the village, she never would have known what it was.

Its beauty was haunting, but she was glad to leave it and all its painful secrets behind.

⸎

When the raft finally reached the other side of the Salt Sea, Avery slipped the ring off her finger, as promised, and handed it to the man, who watched indifferently as she gathered her sack and continued into the night.

"Be careful," Avery thought she heard the young man whisper as she stepped ashore.

It was too late for that, and home was just a few more miles away.

She couldn't decide what she would tell her father first, but it was time to choose.

chapter 30

Attacked

As the hour grew late, Avery wished she had kept at least a morsel of her food—even an apple. She came to a small village where the heavenly fragrance of wood smoke and roasting meat made her stomach ache with emptiness.

Don't stop.

She pushed through her weakness, forcing herself through deep woods until she slowed at the sight of a horse tied to a tree. Soon she found a man sitting on the back of his wagon eating a loaf of bread. The wagon was overloaded with every imaginable household good.

Maybe he knows Father.

"Hello, dear!" he called, his smile broadening in the lamplight that made his face ghostly white. "Come closer so I can get a better look at you!" He saluted her with a bottle, and Avery could only imagine what he was drinking, certain she could already smell his breath from where she stood.

Maybe her attempt to look older had been more successful than she knew. Still, she didn't like the way he eyed her.

Keep walking.

"Wait," the peddler said, his voice kinder. "What do you

need? I can help."

Avery hesitated. She couldn't deny she was weak from hunger, and despite his slurring speech and the promise of his bitter breath, his smile showed he was perhaps friendly.

She turned slowly. "I could use a bite."

The man laughed. "I ain't no cook, little lady, but I can sell you a host o' pots." He gestured grandly toward his merchandise.

Avery shook her head. "No, thank you."

"How about a new dress?"

Avery turned and began walking faster.

She heard him clamber off the wagon and she tried to run, but she was sore and weighed down by the cloak.

He grabbed her and spun her around, bottle still in hand.

"Don't walk away when I'm talking to you!" he spat, his smile gone. "No woman is allowed to disrespect me, especially one so young."

The words struck fear to Avery's heart. If he caught sight of the star on her wrist, he would surely take advantage of the bounty.

"I don't want any pots," Avery said evenly, "and I have no money. What good is a penniless girl to a peddler?"

His laugh sent chills up her spine. "You're wearin' a dress like that and you have no money? You think I'm a fool?"

He threw back a ragged drink, tossed his bottle aside, and yanked her cape from her neck. The strings bit into her skin before ripping away, and she was sure she was bleeding, though she wouldn't dare lift her wrist to check.

With his eyes trained on hers, he dug into the pockets and, finding nothing, circled Avery, still clinging to the cloak.

"Now you've made me angry," he whispered.

"Sell the cloak. You'll make good money on it."

He grabbed her pillowcase and rummaged through it, making Avery glad for the first time that she did not have her mother's necklace.

He shoved her toward his wagon and demanded she climb in. Her legs felt like jelly, but she obeyed. What choice did she have?

He followed, made her sit down, and sat across from her. "What's your name?" he asked.

When she didn't respond, he grabbed her loosened braid and jerked her head back. Bringing his face to within inches of hers and sending a spray of spittle across her face, he said, "Answer me when I ask you a question, understand?"

Avery nodded her throbbing head, and he let go.

"I know how to make you talk," he said. "Don't move."

He turned and began rummaging through a wooden box, and Avery could only imagine what he was after. *A knife? A rope? Worse?*

She wasn't about to sit there and find out. It was now or never. She leapt over the side of the wagon, landing hard on her hands and knees.

As she scrambled to her feet, she saw the man's discarded bottle gleaming in the moonlight and she grabbed it.

"You're a dead girl!" he raged as he staggered to the side of the wagon, the shining blade of a jeweled dagger proof of his promise. He slung one leg over and then the other. Just as his boot reached the ground and he began to pivot, Avery leaned forward and smashed the bottle against the back of his head with all of her might, and he slumped against the wagon and onto the ground in a heap.

For a second Avery stood paralyzed.

She waited for him to stand and come after her, but the man didn't make a sound.

She couldn't risk his coming to, so she gathered up her cape and pillowcase and turned to leave. Then she had another idea. Quickly and carefully she moved to stand over the man's body. His eyes were wide and staring.

Her breath came fast and shallow.

She reached down and slid the jeweled dagger out of his hand.

This might be useful.

Dropping the dagger in her pillowcase, she untied the man's horse—now dancing on the spot—pulled herself onto its back, dug her heels into its flanks, and never looked back.

Cold, tired, hungry, none of that mattered anymore. Reuniting with her father—and hopefully Henry—and spending the night in her own bed drove her on.

No punishment would be worse than this night.

❧

She stopped twice for directions—once in a tiny cluster of peasants' huts and once at a camp of tents—before she recognized her surroundings and knew she was finally close to home.

Nothing had ever felt so good.

She slowed the horse to a trot as she emerged from the woods and reached the edge of the field that separated her from her house—small and plain and glowing against the dark sky.

Stopping, Avery threw her legs over the side and slid to the ground. She tied the horse to a tree and started across the field alone, eager to enjoy every step. She wanted to move faster than her aching body allowed her to go.

Wind whipped through the tall grass and blew her hair around her face. She glanced up at the smoke puffing from the chimney until she stood only a few feet from her front door.

A light drew her to her bedroom window, so she went and peered inside, having dreamed of this moment since she had been snatched from the woods.

Her room was nearly the same as she had left it. It was messier than she remembered, but her brown everyday dress still lay crumpled on the floor, her copy of *Jane Eyre* splayed on the tiny desk beside her bed.

But then she saw the most curious thing.

Someone lay sleeping in her bed. And it wasn't her father or brother.

chapter 31

#

All Avery wanted was to fall into her father's arms and to know that Henry was safe, then sleep till noon in the warmth of her own bed.

And now this.

A dirty man is drooling on my pillow!

She tiptoed back to the front of the cottage, frantic to stay in the shadows, and peered in the window. Six strange men sat at the kitchen table in her family's chairs and ate from her mother's best dishes.

Her father would've called them "dodgy," these men with dirty hands and faces, beards long and unkempt. They ate fast and chewed with their mouths open—food spilling onto their clothes—and one, as soon as he was finished, flung his bowl against the wall. It shattered, prompting the others to burst into raucous belly laughs.

Instinctively, she reached into her pillowcase and retrieved the dagger.

With her back against the house and the dagger at her side, she inched along the home's exterior slowly. Step by nerve-racking step, she prayed that what she found behind the house would confirm her greatest hope and not verify her worst fear.

But when she reached the back of the house, her heart sank and her breath caught in her throat.

The garden was badly overgrown.

Where Avery expected to see her father's straw-covered rows, instead, withered stalks stood bent against the winter weather. He never would have allowed his garden to fall to ruin if he had been home. His carrier pigeons were nowhere to be found.

The realization made her skin go cold and then hot and then cold again.

I risked my life and maybe Henry's life, too, to come home to squatters!

My father is not here and has not been here for a long time!

With a sickening feeling, Avery realized she was no closer to finding her family and had nowhere to go. It wasn't as if she could return to the castle. She had traded everything for this moment, and she had chosen the wrong hand.

And then a thought struck her that she could no longer ignore.

Maybe I am an orphan.

She thought again of the old woman's words in the woods—

"Didn't want to mess with digging another grave."

Maybe the grave had been for her father or Henry. *Or both.*

Something compelled her to go inside. It made no sense, but she could not ignore the feeling.

She knew even before she lifted the handle on the back door that what she was doing was dangerous and stupid, but she had to do it. She needed to see her home one more time, to breathe its familiar scent and linger in its familiar places. She might never be back again.

Seeing her home might help her understand if her father had ever returned after she and Henry were snatched from the woods.

She could hear the men in the kitchen as she quietly closed the back door behind her.

Everything became dark, but she knew the way.

Carefully, she inched along the hall and up the steps. Avoiding her bedroom because of Drooling Man, she sneaked into her father's room where he had built a beautiful bed as a wedding gift for her mother. This was the place where she had curled beside her mother while listening to the best stories about the castle.

The bed was too large and too fancy for their simple, tiny home, but it was stunning—the nicest thing they owned. The blankets were rumpled, and Avery suspected one of the dodgy men downstairs was helping himself to a place to sleep each night.

Nothing in the room gave Avery any reason to believe her father had come home after she and Henry had been taken from the woods.

She saw her father's writing desk, and an idea came to her.

I'll leave a message, and if he returns before I do, he'll know where to go.

She took a step toward the desk as the sound of footsteps approached in the hall.

She squatted beside the bed.

Slow, deliberate steps sounded in the room, followed by a

thud on the mattress.

Crouching, she waited for snoring to come, and then she inched around the mattress and out the bedroom door.

More voices from the kitchen. More laughter.

No time to leave a note.

Breathless and scared, she went back down the stairs and out the back door.

She wanted to cry, but she knew if she started she would never stop. And the star on her wrist left a bounty on her head. She needed shelter, food, and sleep. She would need strength to decide what to do next. And besides the men who had invaded her childhood home, what other evil might lurk in the woods?

Is the old woman looking for me now?

The last place she wanted to wind up was in the Forbidden City.

Avery tightened her grip on the dagger and studied the ground, trying to come up with any option other than heading back across the field. But without help, there was no way she could challenge the half-dozen men in the kitchen and the one in her bedroom.

Where will I go? she prayed. *Please help me.*

She made her way back to the front of the house to leave the way she had come when the front door swung open and she whirled in surprise. One of the men was coming out, and the others were rising from the kitchen table behind him.

"A spy!" the man shouted. "Grab her!"

With the pillowcase still tucked under her arm and the dagger in her hand, Avery hiked up the hem of her cape and lit out across the field.

"After her!"

"She's fast! Get the rifle!"

Avery zigzagged in the darkness, trying to forget her pain and fatigue, hoping she could put enough distance between herself and the men to give her time to untie the horse and leap aboard before they overtook her.

Their voices seemed to fade as she ran, but she couldn't resist peeking back to make sure. Big mistake. Avery didn't know what tripped her, but suddenly she was flat on her face, and the sound of the men's heavy boots grew louder.

She scrambled up and was off again, but her speed and terror spooked the horse, and he skittered and stutter-stepped, circling away from her as she untied him. She cooed, "Whoa, boy, easy, easy," trying to leap astride him.

If only I knew his name!

The men were nearly upon her, but they were gasping and wheezing.

"Come 'ere, you little rapscallion! We'll 'ave you for dessert!"

But now she was aboard the horse and snapped the reins, shouting, "Let's go!" and she bolted away. At the explosive report of a rifle shot, the steed lurched and nearly threw her, but Avery held tightly as the stallion darted through the thick trees.

She didn't slow him until she was certain the men had given up on the chase. Avery patted the horse and murmured in his ear, "I'm going to call you Refuge. You saved my life, old boy."

She led Refuge through familiar territory until she came to the castle made of fruitwood. Avery tied him and was about to enter the elaborate tree house when she heard short, anxious breaths like her own while traveling over the hills.

Avery had no more energy to fight.

If someone discovered her now, she would accept her fate, even welcome it.

Holding her breath in the darkness, she edged toward the play castle when something rushed her, nearly knocking her over, making Refuge whinny.

"Bronte?" she whispered, dropping to her knees to scratch the dog's ears and bury her face in the matted fur. Her pet was the closest thing to family she had seen since she had been carted out of these very woods.

And now they were both strays.

This dog was all she had.

With Bronte at her heels, Avery stepped across the threshold and climbed to the highest point before stretching out on the floor, her head on the dog's back. Exhausted, lonely, and hungry, she once would have been terrified that the shadows in the woods would come alive once her eyes closed.

But not tonight.

The warmth of her furry companion brought her some comfort, and she fell fast asleep in the castle her father had built, sheltered by huge familiar trees, missing those she loved more than ever.

Snap!

Avery awoke to the sound of someone just outside her tree castle.

Crunch.

The sounds were loud and too distinct for an animal.

It took a second for her to realize light shone through the windows of the play castle and morning had arrived. The hunger pains that twisted her stomach confirmed the fact.

Easing the dagger from her pillowcase, Avery moved quietly to the watchtower window and looked down on a young man pacing, staring at his boots.

She couldn't defend herself against a strong young man like this, but whoever he was, he easily could have entered the play castle if he wanted to. The fact that he waited meant maybe he didn't intend to hurt her.

He turned to take another pace, and Avery caught sight of his face. Though she had never spoken to him, she knew instantly who he was.

chapter 32

The Return

"Edward?" Avery called out.

The young man looked up with an impish grin, his cheeks red from the cold.

Avery quickly descended the stairs, Bronte on her heels. She had a sudden urge to hug him but refrained. She hardly knew him, though his name had been on the tip of her tongue since the night he disappeared.

"What are you doing here? Are you okay? How did you get here?"

Edward held up a hand. "I could ask you the same, but there will be no questions until we eat."

Eat! The word was music to her ears.

Dizzy from hunger, Avery looked around for any sign of food but did not find anything.

"Follow me."

Avery slipped the jeweled dagger into the pocket of her dress and followed Edward deeper into the woods. They stopped at a tiny clearing in the thickets where Avery and Henry used to play together.

Avery gasped.

In the center of the clearing was a short, round table, presumably created out of tree stumps, and covered in elaborate tablecloths that had belonged to her mother. A tall, unlit candle stood sentinel to the plates of food.

She didn't ask for an explanation. She didn't request permission. She sat and ate eagerly. The stale bread and cold mushroom soup were not her usual breakfast, but today they were as good as anything she had tasted in the castle.

"Thank you!" she managed around a mouthful. "Did I look that hungry?"

Edward laughed. "Trust me, I remember how starved I was my first night here."

Avery swallowed. "Your first night *here*? In my woods?" That sounded ridiculous, even to her.

Edward shook his head. "Not exactly. You always talked about how wonderful your home was, so when I left the castle, I went in search of it. Hope you're not mad."

When did I tell Edward about my home?

Avery set her food down.

"You *chose* to leave? You weren't forced?"

Edward nodded.

"You weren't sent to the Forbidden City?"

He laughed. "If I had been sent to the Forbidden City, I wouldn't be sitting here with you. You don't leave the Forbidden City."

"Edward! Everyone is worried sick about you, and Ilsa hasn't been herself—"

"Is that a bad thing?" he asked with a chuckle. But when Avery didn't laugh, he cleared his throat and averted his gaze.

"Why did you leave?" she asked, taking a sip of lukewarm coffee.

"Same reason you did, I suspect."

Avery bristled. "And you're staying at my house?"

"Well, not anymore. I distracted the men from following you, and now they aren't happy with me. I'll go back tonight and beg their forgiveness. I do the cooking, so they'll accept my apology." He smiled. "And I'm hoping you'll come with me. They'll eventually warm to the idea of a girl being part of our effort."

"Who are *they*?"

Edward kicked at a rock. "It's better I not tell you yet, but I'm safe and happy. And I'm hoping you will be, too. Tell me why you are here."

"I left the castle because I thought my father was home. Now I have nowhere to go."

Edward looked embarrassed. "That's it? You didn't leave to join the effort?"

Avery shook her head. "I don't even know what you're talking about." Fat white snowflakes began dusting the ground and collecting in their hair. "What am I going to do?" she continued. "Winters here can be brutal, leaving people to hunker down for weeks. No way I can survive in my play castle for long."

Edward extended his hand, and she let him help her up. When she stood, he didn't let go. "There is another option," he said. "Join me."

"Where? How would we survive?"

"We'd have each other," he said, quickly looking away. "We could start our own home, and then, if we're discovered or if a battle breaks out as it's rumored to happen, we could survive it together. I'm confident I could protect you."

Avery had a sudden image of the country brides with their daisy-chain crowns.

She yanked her hand away. "Are you asking me to marry you?"

Edward's face flushed, and he pawed at the ground with the toe of his boot.

"Marriages of convenience are made all the time," he said. "You have nowhere to go, and I'm offering you safety."

"You don't even know me," she continued. "We've never even talked before."

"I used to watch you. Not in a weird way. It was my job to guard the vents. I saw you and Kate explore the castle. I heard you talk about your past and your plans. I watched you in the library. I know your mother's stories. Who do you think notified Tuck every time you got in trouble?" He looked her in the eyes. "I was almost always near you. It was my job. Did you not know?"

Avery shook her head.

But she remembered Kate once telling her she was never more than ten feet from a scout. Apparently she had always been ten feet from Edward, specifically.

"I've come here every day hoping you might show up," he said. He reached again for her hand, but Avery quickly brushed a strand of hair from her face.

I can't marry Edward. I don't care if the other option is being alone.

Another name and another face were imprinted on her heart.

Tuck was honorable. He led by example and acted with wisdom and integrity older than his age. He was kind to everyone and sought solutions where others only saw problems.

"And apparently I have been hoping for something that was never mine to hope for," Edward said. "Let's go back to the castle, then," he said, resignation in his tone. "I suppose you're right that Ilsa deserves to know I'm alive."

"Everyone does," Avery said. "But first I need to show you something."

She led Edward back to the play castle where she retrieved her pillowcase. She pulled out her pages of notes and handed them to him. "You watched Angelina. What did you discover? What facts have I left off this list?"

Edward read the pages carefully.

For a moment, Avery was certain he would give her nothing, making this entire trip home a waste of time. But then he said quietly, "You are right that Angelina and Elizabeth are sisters. Angelina's older sister was the first queen. Angelina was only able to force her way onto the throne because she knows secrets that could jeopardize the future of the entire kingdom, and the king knows it."

"Tell me the secrets."

"I wish I could. I don't know them. I do know it has only ever been Angelina's goal to rule the kingdom, not as the wife of the king, but as the sovereign. She wasn't content being the younger sister and the closest adviser to the most powerful woman. Her older sister stood in the way, and so she had her sister *discarded*."

That word again.

"I thought Elizabeth died in childbirth."

Edward glanced both ways before saying in a quiet voice, "She died *after* childbirth. She was fine one moment and gone the next. Rumor was, she died of a broken heart after learning that something was wrong with her child."

"What was wrong with her child?"

"I don't know. But now the only one who stands in Angelina's way is the king. And he is sick."

"So the king is not the one we should fear?"

Edward nodded. "He may not know it, but his life is in jeopardy more because of Angelina than his illness."

Avery nodded. This was a good start.

"One more thing," Edward said, pointing to a section of Avery's notes. "You're wrong about the old woman. She has never been your enemy. She cared for Queen Elizabeth until her dying day. If you can get the old woman to talk to you, you may discover some of the castle's deepest secrets."

"Thank you."

"Now we need to get you back to the castle. Queen Angelina's coronation was this morning, so the doors will remain unlocked until sundown. If anyone can get you back inside, I can."

The thought of Angelina sitting in the ancient coronation chair draped in the royal coronation robes made Avery's stomach clench. Angelina was one step closer to getting everything she wanted.

The time to act was now.

Avery looked toward the woods in the direction of her home.

She couldn't imagine abandoning her search for her father and Henry now. But what choice did she have? She had nowhere to live, and the castle might actually need her help. She had important information for the cabinet. They needed to know about the threat on the king's life. They needed to find the entrance to the tunnels. She needed to talk to the old woman.

One thing Avery would not do—leave Bronte a second time, especially having no idea whether she would ever return to these woods.

Edward seemed to be watching her with gentle eyes, despite that she had turned down his offer, and she was pleased to see only kindness on his face. He patted his leg, and Bronte joined them.

Avery cleared her throat. "Before we go, I need you to know it means a lot to me that you asked me to stay with you. No one has ever cared for me like that before."

Edward snorted. "You're kidding, right? Half the boys in that castle would offer marriage if you let them, including *him*."

Avery didn't have to ask whom he meant.

Avery told Edward how she had come by Refuge as he hoisted her up onto the horse and then joined her. Bronte followed as they started back to the castle.

Strangely, the castle seemed to be calling her back.

And she was eager to go.

chapter 33

The Deadly Blunder

Avery made sure Edward was careful on their trip back to the castle. In broad daylight, they had to take side roads and stopped briefly only twice.

First, Edward bought warm croissants and fresh cheese from a street vendor. Avery ate gratefully without asking where he got the money to pay for them.

She accepted a news bulletin from a young woman in a head scarf, but when she read it, Avery clasped a hand to her mouth. A blind old woman had been discovered in the village with the first queen's pearls and had been hanged at dawn.

"I gave her those," Avery whispered, but when Edward demanded an explanation, Avery could only shake her head. Leaving the castle had cost at least two people their lives, and the day wasn't over.

Another story in the bulletin—involving the king—might prove useful back at the castle, so Avery folded the page and slipped it into her pillowcase.

The only other time they stopped was to drink from a freshwater stream.

As Refuge and Bronte slurped, and she and Edward scooped

the winter water in cupped hands, Avery said, "You said you saw me reading in the library."

Edward nodded, looking embarrassed again.

"What happened in there? Hundreds of books were ripped from the shelves. Who did it? What book were they looking for?"

Edward shook his head. "A small band posing as staff ransacked the east walls in many rooms throughout the castle. I don't think it had anything to do with a book. My guess is they were looking for a door, some secret access to who knows what."

The passage that connects the castle to the tunnels—it must be in the library.

"Come back to the castle with me," she said. "I am so close to getting so many answers. Together, we could figure everything out."

Edward's eyes grew dark. "I can't."

"What's keeping you out here? Stop trying to protect me. Tell me the truth."

Edward looked both ways before whispering, "A band of soldiers is beginning to form with plans to overthrow the king once and for all. Many of the soldiers once served as staff in the castle before Angelina turned them away. If we can overthrow the king before he has a recognized heir, then Angelina has no rights to the throne when he's gone."

Avery stared at Edward before whispering, "You could be killed for treason!"

"I am inviting you to be on the winning side of history," he continued.

"But what do you mean by *overthrow*?"

Edward averted his gaze.

By late morning, because of the speed of the horse, Avery and Edward were within half a mile of court. Edward tied Refuge out of sight, and Avery led the dog the rest of the way. Thanks to the throng waiting for a glimpse of the king and queen, they were able to slip back into the stairwell via an access point Avery had known nothing about, looking like some sort of young married couple and not a pair of thirteen-year-olds.

"Thank you for your help, Edward," she said as stoically as possible. "Be careful, and take good care of Refuge." She turned to leave, but Edward grabbed her wrist.

"You still have time to change your mind," he whispered. "Come with me, and help us change history."

"I can't," Avery whispered. "I can do more good for our future within these walls."

Edward leaned forward and spoke in Avery's ear. "Not all fairy tales end the way you want them to." He let go of Avery's wrist. "If you change your mind, you know where to find me."

"How will I know if my father ever makes it home?"

"I know where to find *you*. I'll be watching."

Edward reached forward and kissed Avery on the cheek.

Avery sensed a flicker of movement at the top of the stairs and glanced up to see a child darting in the opposite direction.

A scout? No doubt Tuck will be notified of my return before I reach my room.

When Avery looked back, Edward was gone.

She led Bronte to a storage room then stole away to the bunk room to gather blankets and a bowl of water. Hurrying back to make a dog bed, she promised the mutt she would bring food after dinner.

"You've got to be quiet in here," she whispered into Bronte's ear. "I can't get into any more trouble right now." Avery thought the dog somehow understood, considering the tilted head and wagging tail. She scratched the dog's fur and considered what she should do next.

She prayed the dog would be safe—and remain undetected.

And she believed God took interest in the smallest details in life.

⁂

Avery dreaded facing her friends, but even so, she had no idea how upset they would be.

Avery sat on her bed while Kate paced before her.

"Everyone thought you'd been sent to the Forbidden City," Kate said in a tone Avery didn't recognize, her arms crossed tightly over her chest. "Tuck almost left to look for you. He could have died trying to find you."

"I'm sorry," Avery said. "I left the tiara and the ribbon so you'd know it was my choice."

Kate did not respond.

Avery narrowed her eyes. "You didn't tell people I left of my own will, did you? You wanted them to worry."

Kate averted her eyes.

"You wanted Tuck to find me and bring me back, didn't you?" Avery stood and spun Kate around. "*You* are the one who would have risked his life! Why is it so important to you that I stay here?"

Kate's eyes filled and looked past Avery to the door. "I know things," she whispered. "And not everything I know is information I asked to know. You need to stay here for everything to work. You are our only chance of survival."

"Who are you?" Avery burst out. The words escaped her lips before she could stop them.

"I have been put in charge of your safety and well-being."

"By whom?"

Avery never could have prepared herself for the words Kate said next—

"Someone who knows your mother."

Avery learned at supper that Ilsa had been installed as the new child queen. At first, Avery didn't care. She hadn't wanted the title to begin with, but as the reality set in, she couldn't shake the thought that Tuck had wasted no time replacing her with Ilsa, and something even more ominous: *Now I don't belong anywhere.*

Late that night, after Avery had sneaked some good scraps to Bronte when everyone else was participating in a chess tournament, Tuck summoned her to the dining room along with Kendrick, Kate, and Ilsa.

Tuck paced while Kendrick sat, elbows on the table and hands folded. Avery sat next to Kate, stealing worried glances at her and trying to avoid Ilsa's self-satisfied smile at all costs.

"I'm sorry," Avery said, finally breaking the silence. "I shouldn't have left."

"Save your apologies," Tuck said without meeting her eyes.

"You shouldn't have been allowed back either," Ilsa said. "You know that, right? You've jeopardized all of our safety. What if somebody saw you or followed you?"

"But they didn't."

"Not true," Kendrick said, not looking at her. "One of our scouts saw you with Edward on the stairs."

Avery felt the red creep into her neck. She hated the way he had said that.

She hadn't anticipated being interrogated by the entire group. Had the scout told Tuck what Edward had said? Had the scout mentioned that Edward had kissed her on the cheek?

She looked at Ilsa with all the pleading she could muster.

You should be grateful I was on the stairs with Edward. I brought him back!

Ilsa didn't flinch. Her mouth twisted into a bitter smile.

Tuck shook his head and sighed. "You know there must be a public consequence for this. We can't let other kids think they can just leave the castle or break the rules. Doing so could put us all in jeopardy at any time." Despite his words, his voice was gentle, and Avery decided his anger would have been easier to take right now than his kindness.

"Fine," Avery said, eager to end the conversation. "Let me know when you decide what it should be."

"One more thing," Kate said, speaking up for the first time. "The old lady has asked me to remind you that leaving this castle jeopardizes the safety of your brother."

Avery felt her pulse in her neck.

At least I know he's still alive.

"If you leave again," Tuck said, "don't bother coming back." With those words, he stood and left the dining room.

"Tuck, wait!" Avery ran to the door, but by the time she reached the hallway, he was gone.

⌘

Back in the bunk room Avery collapsed on her bed and buried her face in the crook of her arm.

She cried for her family.

She cried for herself.

She cried for Edward.

She cried for Tuck.

She had failed so many people.

When she heard footsteps approach, she assumed Kate had come to sit with her.

"You can have this back. I don't want it."

Avery looked up to see Ilsa, the pearl tiara dangling from her fingers. Embarrassed to be caught crying in front of her, Avery pushed herself up and wiped her face. "Why give it back? We both know you've wanted it since before I arrived."

"I won't be anyone's consolation prize." Ilsa tossed the tiara onto the bed. "Anyway, I got what I wanted."

Avery laughed. "Of course. Seeing me like this."

"Don't give yourself so much credit. What I wanted was one more chance to talk to Edward. Now I know he wanted to leave and wasn't forced to go. He told me you convinced him to speak to me."

Avery had to let that sink in. So something good *had* come from this horrible day?

"I'm glad he—"

"This doesn't make us friends," Ilsa interrupted. "I look forward to seeing whatever price you have to pay for leaving the castle. It was the stupidest thing you've ever done, which is saying a lot." And as quickly as she had entered, she was gone.

And Avery knew she had somewhere she needed to go immediately.

chapter 34

Correspondence Game

Avery stood in the darkened chapel alone.

One by one she lit the candles until the room flickered to life, the light dancing on the gold-gilded walls and illuminating the stained-glass windows. Instead of taking a seat on any of the empty high-back pews, however, she knelt on the crimson carpet in front of the pulpit. She leaned forward until she lay prostrate on the ground, her arms above her head and her face pressed into the carpet. And in the same room where a secession of kings had confidently determined their disbelief in God and vowed never to return to worship, Avery acknowledged her belief.

She asked for wisdom.

She asked for safety.

She *begged* for courage.

And beneath the ceiling where an oppressive mural of the kingdom's darkest stories had been painted to life, Avery sought the face of God, convinced He could use her at such a time as this.

She had said no to Edward for several reasons, not the least of which was something she had read in her Bible on the day before she left the castle.

God sets up kings and removes them.

Choosing to side against God's ordained leadership was choosing to side against God.

❧

Avery was shocked to find a parcel under her pillow.

She had assumed Kendrick was just as mad at her as everyone else seemed to be. He hadn't even looked her direction since she had returned. So this would likely be an angry rant.

Maybe he's written to take back everything he said. I don't blame him.

When Avery was certain the girls in the room were fast asleep, she took a candle and a match from the fireplace and sneaked down the hall to the storage room again.

Bronte greeted her as if she had been gone for a month.

She had to fend the dog off as she lit the candle and opened the envelope with fingers trembling.

But before she could spread the page, Bronte began a high-pitched whine that sent a shiver up Avery's spine. The dog paced near the makeshift dog bed but wouldn't sit.

"What's wrong?" Avery whispered.

She carefully placed the candle in a stand and petted Bronte softly, but Bronte still shook and panted. Avery looked around for any sign of rat poison or anything else amiss. Nothing looked out of place. The food scraps and water appeared untouched.

Did Ilsa do something to Bronte? Is this her revenge?

"What's the matter?" Avery asked, taking Bronte's face in her hands and looking into the deep, dark eyes that looked like wells of ink. Bronte pulled away, agitated. The thought of her dog being sick terrified her. She couldn't lose Bronte, too, especially after everything.

Avery slumped against the wall and watched the dog pace. She was tempted to find Kate, Tuck, or Kendrick, but she couldn't risk their knowing about Bronte, upset as they were with her already.

She would just have to sit and wait.

She retrieved the candle and unfolded the message, steeling herself for whatever she found. To her surprise, it consisted of only two lines:

Why did you come back?
Leave your response under your pillow and it will be delivered.

She had asked herself the same question. The truth was, it was cold outside and she'd had nowhere else to go.

But that wasn't all, and she knew it.

The truth was that she couldn't stand the thought of never seeing Tuck. She missed their conversations, his gentle teasing and confident reassurance. She missed the way he looked out for her, especially when she was about to dive into some foolish decision. She needed his confident leadership in her life.

Avery didn't fully understand her own feelings, but she knew they were real.

And there was something else.

If only for the sake of the other kids, she needed to find the tunnels. They called to her in her dreams. Every night when she slept she worked on their location. She wanted to find them, but not just for the tunnels. What if the underground colonies her mother had talked about were real, too? What if the tunnels were filled with their brothers and sisters?

For now, she would worry only about her beloved Bronte.

⌒⊗⌒

Sometime during the wee hours, the old dog fell into what appeared to be a fragile slumber. Avery draped a blanket over her friend, kissed Bronte's silky head, and tiptoed back to her bed. She couldn't afford to be discovered missing from her bed in the morning and have people assume she had fled the castle again. Neither could she have them come looking for her, only to discover her dog.

Nor did she want to see her dog die. She wasn't sure she was strong enough to handle it.

She needed to reconcile with Tuck and tell him first before anyone else learned about Bronte.

chapter 35

The Misread

With the memory of her hunger in the woods still on her mind, Avery filled her plate at breakfast with meats, potatoes, and sweet breads.

Carefully folding some of the meat in a napkin for Bronte, she was about to dig in when a breathless, excited girl she did not recognize rushed in and announced, "There are dogs in the storage room!"

The room burst into a frenzy of excited conversation.

Dogs?

Avery dropped her fork, pushed back her chair, and flew past the girl down the hall. A crowd had already gathered inside the storage room, and she pushed past them, too.

Bronte lay on the blankets Avery had spread the night before, only now, three puppies nursed beside her.

Avery dropped to her knees and gently stroked the dog's head. "Oh, Bronte, you weren't sick!" she whispered. "You were in labor. How did I miss the signs?"

"Be careful," one of the kids said. "We don't know where she came from. She could have a disease. What if she bites you?"

"Motherhood is not a disease," Avery said, kissing Bronte's head repeatedly.

"Clear the room, please," Tuck said from the door. "Let me take a look at the dog."

Everyone else shuffled out until it was just Tuck and Avery. He knelt and gently cupped Bronte's face in his hands, making Avery wonder if he, too, had left a dog behind.

"How do you think she got in here?" he asked.

"Maybe looking for a warm spot and hoping we would help her?"

"She looks healthy enough," Tuck said. "But she can't stay here. Barking dogs could get us discovered quickly. We need to find a way to let her loose."

"But we make noise, and we haven't been discovered. Anyway, it seems wrong to send her back into the cold with babies. They'll never make it."

Tuck held Avery's gaze for a moment.

"Maybe," he said slowly. Then his eyes widened so that Avery could tell something dawned on him. "You know, we could use a happy distraction around here."

Avery wiped her eyes and wished Tuck would look away. The kindness in his face unnerved her. She wanted so badly to tell him everything—including what had happened in the woods and why she had come back—but it had been a long night, and she just couldn't.

Suddenly, here came Kendrick and Kate.

Kate immediately began mothering Bronte, promising her a warm bath and food.

"And water," Avery said.

"Yes," Kate said. "Giving birth makes mothers dehydrated."

"We'll put the dogs up for a vote," Tuck said. "If the vote is *no*, I'll have no choice but to send her away. If the vote is *yes*, there will need to be rules."

Avery nodded. As long as Bronte was able to stay, she wouldn't tell anyone it was her dog. That could always come later.

Late that night, the kids filed into the great room for "midnight court," as it had come to be known—a mock version of what happened with the real king and queen downstairs. Matters were discussed and announcements were made. Tonight, Tuck sat at the front with an empty chair beside him and a large sheet hanging precariously behind, obviously hiding something from the kids.

He called the meeting to order and announced two items of business, the first being "the matter of the dog we're calling Bronte, and her pups."

Cheers rose from the crowd, and the kids voted unanimously to keep them. Tuck announced that the pups could be named later.

"Another matter of business," he said, his tone serious. "You all have been discussing Avery's decision to leave the castle. I am not at liberty to explain why she made the choice that she did, but it was honorable. As restitution, I officially place Avery in charge of looking after Bronte's well-being. Do you accept this responsibility?"

Avery nodded, but not as vigorously as she felt.

Her heart soared. Tuck was being kind.

"A final matter of business," he said, "is our crest."

Avery's stomach turned. Tuck had asked her to create it ages ago, but since she had sketched it and given it to Kate, she had never followed up on it.

Had she failed Tuck in this matter, too?

He turned to the large sheet behind his chair and, with a flourish, gave it a firm tug. It fell away to reveal a gorgeous silk flag.

Everyone, including Avery, gasped.

In the center lay the black shield, trees with dozens of bright leaves, swirling ribbons with pops of color, and the motto *Viam inveniam aut faciam.*

I will either find a way or make one.

The crest was more beautiful than Avery had thought possible. Kate had sewn exactly what Avery had imagined.

Avery locked eyes with Kate across the room. "Thank you," she mouthed, knowing for the first time since she returned that all would be well between them.

The kids were standing and clapping, and all eyes were on Avery.

Tuck motioned for her to join him. Stunned, she struggled to her feet and moved to stand beside him.

"Where's your tiara?" he asked in her ear as the crowd continued to applaud.

"I wasn't going to wear it until you said I should."

"You should," he said. "You are their queen. Just as you are mine."

chapter 36

𝕭𝖔𝖔𝖐 𝕸𝖔𝖛𝖊

The next day, Avery called her own meeting of the cabinet, asking Kate, Kendrick, and Tuck to meet her in the kids' store before it opened.

The news bulletin she had received while traveling with Edward was burning a hole in her pocket, and since no one had said anything to her about it since she'd returned, she assumed they hadn't yet received the news.

And since she finally felt like their friendship was getting back on track, she knew it was the right time to discuss the matter.

"There's something you need to see," she said, unfolding the paper and reading the headline, " 'The King Has an Heir!' "

Tuck narrowed his eyes, and Kendrick shot her a double take. The king and queen had only recently married, and rumor had it the king eagerly desired an heir. But so soon?

Tuck reached for the bulletin and passed it to Kendrick, who mumbled as he read, " 'King George has acknowledged a child born to his first wife, Elizabeth, who died within hours of her son's delivery. The announcement of the heir to the throne was made after careful deliberation by the king.' "

"I don't get it," Tuck said. "It's no secret that Elizabeth gave birth to a baby boy who died hours later. Why make it important news?"

"Maybe someone is trying to upset Angelina by bringing it up," Kendrick said.

"Then why would the king acknowledge the child now?" Avery asked.

"Maybe the king is afraid he won't have any other heir and is desperate," Tuck offered.

"Or maybe the heir is alive," Avery said. "Maybe they aren't sure, and this is the beginning of a formal search."

All eyes turned to Kate, who, so far, had said nothing.

Turning to Kendrick, Kate asked, "When did Queen Elizabeth die?"

Kendrick shrugged. "I'd have to look it up, but I would guess twelve or thirteen—"

The members of the council looked at each other as the light seemed to dawn on each of them.

Avery finally spoke. "So the king's heir dies or disappears roughly thirteen years ago, and now all thirteen-year-old orphans in the kingdom have been brought to the castle—presumably by Angelina—while she seeks to supply her own heir to the throne? Do we really believe this is a coincidence?"

There was a long, unsteady silence.

"We don't know this has anything to do with us," Tuck finally said carefully.

"But if it does?" Avery asked. "And if this announcement has been made ahead of a formal inquiry and Angelina knows a potential heir exists among us?"

"Then our lives could be in greater danger than we thought," Tuck said. "But why would girls be included? The king lost a son, not a daughter. Until we know facts, we keep this to ourselves, agreed?"

They all nodded.

"The king's heir could be living among us," Kate whispered. "Can you imagine? One of us could be the next—"

"Wait," Kendrick said. "If we're here because the king is looking for his heir, why are we hiding from him?"

"Because we aren't hiding from *him*," Avery said.

Angelina wants to find the heir before the king discovers him.

The pieces were slowly starting to fit. Before they acted on it, though, they needed to be certain. If they were wrong about the king and he did want them discarded, the wrong move could be their undoing.

⌒∞⌒

Later that day, Avery decided it was time for her to respond to Kendrick's messages. She owed him the truth and was determined to write him before she changed her mind.

She sat on her bed, agonizing over what to say.

Words, once on paper, can never be destroyed.

"Dear Friend" seemed too impersonal, but "Dear Kendrick" seemed too presumptuous. He didn't know she had compared handwriting samples and knew who he was.

Thank you for writing me, she began, wishing she had his gift of words. *I have looked forward to your messages since you first began sending them. However, as to why I returned to the castle—*

Just then, Kate burst into the bunk room, wide-eyed and breathless. "Come quickly!"

Avery set her pen and paper aside and followed her friend into the hallway and down the stairs.

"What's going on?"

"I don't know how to tell you. It's all so strange. You need to see it for yourself."

They stopped at a landing. "I know you love the library," Kate said, "but Angelina has decided to clean up the mess by getting rid of all the books. Look!"

Kate pushed open the door to reveal a massive, hissing incinerator that flickered and snapped and belched enough smoke and heat that Avery immediately broke into a sweat and took several steps back. Stacks of old leather books with gold pages and brass clasps stood in piles awaiting their destruction.

"Why is this happening?" Avery asked. "We've got to stop this."

Kate grabbed her arm. "We can't. They'll be back any minute with more."

"Then we need to save what's left upstairs."

Avery didn't wait for Kate's response, but instead raced up the stairwell. She stuck her head into each door, calling for kids to come and help. She saw Kendrick in one of the rooms, and he looked stricken by the news. By the time they arrived at the library, she had recruited over a dozen, but strangely Kendrick wasn't among them.

"When we're certain the adults have left to take a load downstairs," she said, "we'll remove as many books as possible. Don't check titles. Move books to our quarters, and we'll sort them later. Just don't get caught. When I ring the bell, leave immediately. Understand? Nothing matters more than your safety!"

Avery peeked into the library. A group of plainly dressed adults were on their way out the opposite door, balancing stacks of books up to their chins.

She pushed open the door and the kids flooded in, grabbing books from everywhere and carrying them to the kids' quarters.

Avery crossed to the opposite door and peeked outside to the stairwell used by the adults. Thankfully it was made of marble, so when she heard the thunder of footsteps growing louder, she rang a handbell and the kids fled.

They repeated this cycle for most of the afternoon, and throughout the day more kids came to help.

In the end, hundreds of books had been rescued, which kept Avery's mind off the thousands of others that were destroyed.

After thanking the kids, she lingered in the empty room that had once been alive with knowledge, now empty and dark and sad.

And then she saw something on one wall that had been swept of books: a tiny silver keyhole. Edward's words rang in her ears.

My guess is they were looking for a door, some secret access. . . .

"And it's an east-facing wall," she whispered.

Avery pushed and pulled the bare shelf with all her strength, but it would not budge.

She felt foolish, but she would be back. She would not give up until she learned what lay behind the door. She hoped she knew the answer.

⌘

Avery returned to the bunk room to finish her letter to Kendrick.

Soon, Kate came and sat on her own bed next to Avery's.

"You did a good thing today," Kate said quietly, stretching out.

Avery set down her pen, wondering if she would ever be able to finish. "I don't understand why Angelina needed to destroy the books. If she was concerned about the mess, the old woman could have commissioned us to put the books back on the shelves. I would have done it myself."

Kate smiled. "I love how much you love books. It's one of your good qualities. Leaders are readers."

Avery nodded. Her mother had always said the same thing.

"The books never posed a threat to the queen," Avery said. "I doubt she even reads."

"Maybe she wants the library for something else. Maybe she's looking for the same thing you are trying to find."

Avery sighed.

"Be careful," Kate said. "When people around here get close to discovering something, strange things happen to them."

Avery turned back to her letter and began to write.

The sooner she told Kendrick how she felt, the better.

chapter 37

A Win

Nothing, Avery decided, made her hungrier than speaking her mind. After folding her letter to Kendrick neatly in thirds, she slid it under her pillow and went in search of leftovers in the kitchen. Finding little, she settled for apples and chocolate.

In her letter to Kendrick she had explained carefully that she had returned because of a growing friendship with someone in the castle. *I missed him,* she wrote, *and even though I cannot explain it, I had to return.*

She then apologized to Kendrick—though she did not use his name, of course—that she could never think of him as more than a brother and that she was sorry if she had in any way led him to believe otherwise.

She added a simple invitation to meet and discuss it further.

She knew Kendrick would never take her up on a meeting.

He still refused to look her in the eye.

⚜

After going back for bread and cheese, Avery wandered into the storage room containing Elizabeth's possessions, where stacks upon stacks of salvaged books now flooded the space as well. Had they not reminded her of so many more that had been destroyed, the very sight of these things of beauty would have thrilled her.

She paged through random selections on subjects ranging from royal history to science to literature and everything in between. She decided she would create a library in the kids' quarters and encourage her peers to study.

She would ask Tuck to allow her to make a presentation at the next midnight court where she would tell them, "There's no reason we can't go to school! As long as we have books, we have teachers!"

Maybe she would even ask the chaplain to share the verse he had read the previous Sunday. *Let no man despise you because of your youth.*

The next book Avery opened made her blood turn cold.

Inside the cover, inscribed on a wax bookplate, was the name *Godfrey*.

She had a dozen such books in her play castle, so there was no mistaking it. Her father made the bookplates by hand.

Right beneath the bookplate—in her mother's handwriting—came the admonishment: *This book must not be destroyed.*

It was an otherwise nondescript book about travel, but it had belonged to her parents and obviously had been important to her mother. How it had found its way to the castle, Avery had no idea, but she was beginning to suspect her family had deep ties to the castle. She pressed it to her heart.

Maybe it wouldn't hurt if she kept this one for her own collection. She needed to understand its significance.

chapter 38

True Love

Avery sent a note to the old woman via a messenger asking for a meeting.

She could not ignore Edward's instruction—*"If you can get the old woman to talk to you, you may discover some of the castle's deepest secrets."*

While she waited for a reply, she spent hours slowly reading her mother's book, carefully turning each page, wishing—hoping—for some message that might allow it all to make sense. She remembered nothing of this book or her mother saying anything about it, and nothing in the pictures and maps of faraway places brought her any closer to solving the mysteries of the castle.

She scanned the margins for handwritten notes or secret code but found nothing.

She stayed up reading the book until candle after candle burned itself out.

But she wasn't about to give up. Thick and boring as it was, she would see it through to the end.

As she scanned the pages, she allowed her mind to wander to the days following her mother's disappearance and the odd way her father never searched for her.

Avery had peppered the villagers with questions, passing out handwritten flyers and asking everyone she met whether or not they recognized a painting of her mother or had seen her.

The answer had always been the same. No.

Her father never prohibited her from searching, but he had never helped her either.

Her determination to find answers had resulted in endless arguments with her father that she could never win. She would harness that determination now.

⌘

On the second night of waiting for the old woman's reply, Avery was surprised to discover a message under her pillow. Eagerly she opened it, hoping the old woman had agreed, and was even more surprised that it was from Kendrick, asking her to meet tomorrow after breakfast in the great room.

Of course she would meet him. The sooner this was finished, the better.

Things had grown only stranger between her and Kendrick. Each time she tried talking to him, he grew uncomfortable and walked away. He hadn't even come to help rescue the books in the library, which made no sense seeing he loved them as much as she did. Maybe now they could talk openly and get their friendship back on track.

In the morning, Avery dressed in the newest gown Kate had given her—an emerald dress that shimmered when she walked.

She brushed her hair into a smooth knot at the base of her neck—believing it made her look more intelligent and hopefully even a tad remorseful.

"There is usually something you can apologize for in any hurtful situation," her mother had always encouraged her. And especially where Kendrick was involved, this was true.

After breakfast she lingered, silently rehearsing what she would say. *I want us to be friends, to be able to talk about books and castle news like we once did. We need to stick together here in these walls to save our lives. We can do that, right?*

She wished she'd told Kate about the meeting and had sought her advice.

The hundred feet or so between the dining room and the great room felt like miles.

I want us to be friends, to be able to talk about books and castle news.

She rehearsed the words until she was confident they would roll off her tongue.

When she arrived, there he stood, tall and broad shouldered, but *not* Kendrick.

"Tuck?"

Avery looked to see if Kendrick was close by. Maybe Kendrick had invited him. The two were usually inseparable. She didn't want to have this conversation in front of Tuck.

"Yes," Tuck said. But his normal look of confidence had been replaced by uncertainty, those green eyes full of something Avery had never seen.

As he approached, Avery realized Kendrick wasn't coming.

"But it was Kendrick's handwriting," she blurted. "I compared it to another sample."

Tuck laughed as red crept into his cheeks. He looked at the floor. "I can't write."

An orchestra of cymbals collided in Avery's head. "You what?"

"Or read, actually. It's embarrassing, but I never learned."

Avery shook her head, speechless.

"I asked Kendrick to write for me. He thought the poetry was ridiculous and avoided you like the plague, but I made him write it anyway. You did receive the poetry, didn't you? I hope he wrote what I said."

Avery nodded. "But I had no idea it was from you."

"What do you think I was trying to tell you on the watch turret when we had our picnic?"

Avery stared, words abandoning her. She had been preoccupied that day.

"I got your reply about being brother and sister," Tuck continued. "That's fine. I understand."

"Being friends is good," she managed.

"Just one question, then," Tuck said, "since we're friends—"

Avery nodded again.

"Who is it you care so much for, the one for whom you returned to the castle?"

Avery shrugged and looked away, feeling the heat in her own face now.

This conversation was not going as planned.

Tuck ducked his head, forcing her to look him in the eye.

"You believed you were writing Kendrick, so who were you talking about? Was it Edward? It would explain your conversation on the stairs and why you left."

A pause the length of the Salt Sea made Avery think of a thousand things she should say. But if she had learned nothing else from this entire ordeal, it was that truth mattered above all.

"You," she choked. She wanted to say more, but she couldn't.

She tried to swallow, but the room began to spin, and she couldn't hold his knowing gaze. Neither could she fight the urge to flee.

Avery turned and hurried away, leaving Tuck standing there alone.

chapter 39

Sudden Death

Avery and Kate were sorting items in the kids' store the next day when a shaken girl appeared in the doorway. "The old woman is dead!"

"What are you talking about?" Avery asked.

"She was working downstairs and just fell over."

Kate dropped the glass bowl in her hands, sending shards of glass in every direction. She turned and ran for the hall, and Avery followed.

The girl led them to one of the bunk rooms on the boys' side where Kendrick was waiting for them. Together they knelt over a metal grate in the floor, and he cranked open the slats.

Sure enough, the old woman lay on the floor below, eyes wide and staring.

Adult staff gathered around the body and talked in hushed tones. Something about the situation seemed wrong, but Avery couldn't determine what it was.

No panic. No surprise. No sadness.

The adults agreed they should say the woman had died of heart failure, and soon another arrived with a blanket and covered her body. The group of adults skittered away, talking quietly among themselves.

Kendrick shut the grate.

"Now we won't get any more answers from her," Avery said. "We're on our own."

"Not necessarily," Kendrick said, adjusting his glasses. "Let's see if she receives a memorial or any mention in the news bulletin. Maybe we'll learn more about her than we would otherwise."

"Do you think she died of natural causes?" Avery asked.

"No," Kendrick said, "but I don't know who would have killed her or why. We should learn who would profit the most from her death. Why would someone want the old woman dead?"

Avery couldn't shake the thought: *I requested a meeting with her. Someone didn't want her talking to me. This is my fault.*

"She knew too much," Kendrick continued. "Maybe she was planning to tell the truth."

Avery's blood turned to ice. She changed the subject—

"What will we do without a direct adult link in the castle? How will we know what tasks need to get done?"

Kendrick shrugged, and for the first time since they'd met, he startled Avery by looking directly at her. For a moment, Avery couldn't speak. Her mouth hung open, but no words came. She finally forced herself to ask a question so the situation would return to normal.

"What could she possibly know that would jeopardize her life?"

Kate spoke. "She knew more about the king's first wife than anyone alive. She cared for Queen Elizabeth and the newborn heir."

Exactly as Edward said.

Then she would have recognized the necklace I was wearing in the woods. She would have known it belonged to Elizabeth. Did that necklace mark me?

Kendrick closed the grate, and in that moment the oddest thing happened. Perfectly poised Kate burst into full, body-racking sobs. Holding her stomach, she bent forward and allowed the grief to swallow her whole, hot tears coursing down her cheeks and pooling on the floor.

Avery grabbed her arm. "Kate!"

In a strange reversal of events, she held her friend the same way Kate had held her on the first night in the castle.

But Kate would not be comforted. Not until Avery helped her to her bed did the crying stop, but she never offered an explanation. In one afternoon, Kate the wise young woman became Kate the sad young girl, and Avery stood guard at Kate's bedside to watch over her.

Once Kate was sleeping soundly, Avery pulled out her pages of handwritten notes.

In addition to Kate's unusual behavior, Tuck had notified the council that he wanted to interview each thirteen-year-old to see if any immediate connections surfaced with Queen Elizabeth. He wanted to be proactive at locating a possible heir among them without the kids knowing what he was doing.

Avery suspected now, though, the interviews were unnecessary.

With pen in hand, she added Kendrick's eyes to her list of mysterious castle facts:

One is brown and the other blue.

The old woman did not receive a memorial, nor any mention in the news bulletin. Once her body was removed from the castle, she was gone, literally and figuratively—along with any hope of knowing more of her secrets. Subsequently, the castle door to the outside world—the one she used to transport children—was bolted shut.

Several days after her death, the king and queen again traveled on business.

With a scout posted at the gallery door, Avery worked on the theme song for the Olympiad. She had spent several nights tossing and turning, humming and making notes.

She was unhappy with everything she tried. Nothing seemed worthy of the event.

Most of her creative sessions ended in a snowstorm of wasted parchment and promises to never play music again.

Now, back at the organ, Avery took a deep breath.

"When you face a problem," her mother had always said, *"begin with what you know."*

And so she warmed up with something her parents had created, a simple tune they paired with whatever lyrics struck them at the time. Sometimes they used it to sing of going to sleep, at other times to sing of cleaning the house or pulling weeds in the garden. They had used the tune for every occasion since Avery was a little girl.

She was certain the tune never belonged to the first queen because it had evolved over the years as the lyrics changed. The tune brought a smile to her, and soon she was ready to try composing again, hoping to write a song worthy of the greatest games on earth.

❦

When the king and queen returned, word spread through the castle that the king had an important announcement.

A new heir on the way? Avery wondered as she made her way to a grate that overlooked the Great Hall. *Will Angelina finally receive her wish? Will this put an end to the madness? Is this the moment history will be written?*

Kate was waiting at the grate when Avery arrived, her face sad and swollen. She was wearing an uncharacteristically plain black dress.

They knelt to wait for the news.

"Are you okay?" Avery whispered.

"There is something you should know," Kate said. "But you must promise me you will never speak of it to anyone."

"Of course."

"The old woman was my grandmother."

Avery's eyes grew wide. Kate was wearing the black mourning gown.

Her mind began racing.

If Kate was the granddaughter of the old woman, Kate had grown up in the castle—or at least made frequent visits. No wonder she had so many answers. No wonder she *knew things*.

She probably knows far more than she's admitted.

"I've been waiting for the right moment to tell you," Kate continued.

"Are you an orphan?" Avery asked.

Kate nodded.

"Are you thirteen?"

Slowly, Kate shook her head.

Something between them shifted with this shared knowledge.

Avery wanted to ask questions—a million of them—but crowds gathered below, pushing in around the king's throne, and excited voices rose. Soon a flourish of trumpets sounded and the beaming king appeared to low bows and enthusiastic applause.

Avery found herself giddy.

The king thanked everyone for coming, and—like the kids throughout the castle—the crowd seemed to hang on his every word.

"I am excited to announce that the Olympiad is close at hand. I have decreed that all residents of the kingdom—from the oldest to the youngest—shall be free to attend. No one will be denied entrance into the greatest games on earth. For this one moment in our history, we will set aside rank, and all classes will be free to cheer on our contestants side by side. I want you all to be there!"

He raised a gold cup as the crowd cheered wildly.

"Age will not matter. Wealth will not matter. Men and women, boys and girls are welcome."

Again the crowd erupted, and Avery heard the clanging of

bells and the cheering from outside the castle walls.

Kate clapped the grate closed.

"What are you doing?" Avery asked. "I want to hear the rest! This is good news!"

"When will you understand that nothing with this king and queen is that simple? It's got to be a trap. Angelina has encouraged him to invite everyone so that *she* can find someone."

Avery looked into Kate's sad eyes.

She would not say it now, but it was a risk she was willing to take.

The need to stay in the castle was strong, but the need to find her family was stronger.

When the Olympiad opened, she would be there, with or without Kate's approval.

chapter 40

The Idea

Tuck and Avery hadn't spoken since their surprise meeting in the great room.

Tuck smiled as she approached, and when they were finally alone in the dining room, he pulled out a chair for her.

"Thank you for meeting with me," she said quietly, trembling.

"I'm glad you asked," he said, his eyes as alarming to her as the first time she saw them. "I'm glad to see you still wear the ring."

Avery looked down at the crown ring he had given her at Christmas.

She winced, knowing what she was about to do.

"Before you tell me why you wanted to meet, I have news," Tuck began. "Intelligence has notified me that an army is beginning to form in the village with plans to overthrow the king."

A lump formed in Avery's throat. She knew this because of her conversation with Edward, but revealing this to Tuck would harm the fragile thread between them.

"If they can gather enough soldiers, everyone in this castle will be in danger," Tuck continued. "If we get caught in the crosshairs of a rebellion, we will fight for our survival like everyone else. It's another reason we need to find a safer place to live. And without the old woman to tell us what to do, our security is in jeopardy."

"The underground colonies," Avery said. "It's my first priority. I am so close."

Tuck nodded. "Good. Now, what did you want to talk to me about?"

"I'm here to ask you to place a spy in court."

"Go on."

"A spy could get closer to Angelina, see how she spends her time, learn what she thinks and plans, and listen in on her meetings and conversations from a better vantage point than we are given from the grates."

"How would it work? Angelina doesn't let anyone get close to her."

"Every time I see her, a dozen ladies trail in service, planning her wardrobe or creating her seating charts. She doesn't sneeze without the presence of an audience. Place a spy among those ladies and she'd never know."

Avery could see that Tuck liked the idea.

"Who do you think is ideal for the task?" he asked.

"Me."

Tuck started to protest, but Avery put up a hand. "Hear me out," she said. "I'm so close to putting everything together, and I know the missing pieces I must find. Allowing someone else to do this will slow things down, and as you just said, we don't have time."

"If something happened to you, I could never forgive myself."

"I know. Which is why I must give this back for now."

Carefully she twisted off the castle ring and held it out to him. "I want to wear it," she said, "but not yet. I need you to keep it for now."

"Why?"

"Queens are never permitted to put the personal above the political."

Tuck nodded, confusion in his eyes. He swallowed hard before accepting the ring. "I will keep it safe until you want it back. And I will trust that you will ask for it back someday."

Avery nodded. "I will."

A heavy silence passed between them.

When Tuck remained quiet, Avery continued. "You said you could never forgive yourself if something happened to me, but if we never find our way out of here, I could never forgive *myself*. Promise you'll think about it."

When Tuck nodded, Avery put her hand on his.

It was a start.

⚬≪∞≫⚬

Everyone in the kingdom was abuzz preparing for the Olympiad only a few months away.

Avery went to work writing out the score for the song she had arranged. It was simple and not at all what she had dreamed of. But she believed it would make the king happy.

On sheets of parchment with the edge of a knife she drew the horizontal lines and spaces that represented the musical staff. She carefully dipped her pen in a jar of ink from Kendrick's desk and colored in the notes. She could hear the score in her head as she worked.

Finished, she took the music to Tuck, who congratulated her and told her that he couldn't wait to hear what she had created.

It was good to be done.

She had embellished the tune her parents had created to make it appropriate for the occasion. Maybe, just maybe, if her father came within earshot of the Olympiad, he would recognize the song and know where to find her.

She could always hope.

With so much at stake, these really could be the greatest games on earth.

CHAPTER 41

The Opening

Late that night, Avery lay on her bed flipping the pages of her mother's travel book, still wondering why her mother had written that it "must not be destroyed."

It still looked like an ordinary travel guide.

Avery was thankful, at least, that the task of reading it was almost finished. She would rather spend a day bartering over marbles and castle castoffs than to ever read about currency exchanges again. The book did not seem the type her mother would have considered a favorite, having always favored dreamy fairy tales and fables.

Finishing, Avery debated scanning the index, but the book had been dull enough without lists of archaic names from obscure countries.

Keep looking, the pages seemed to say.

So she fanned the pages quickly, seeing nothing.

But she felt something.

Something hard and out of place in the back of the book. The thick back cover had been hollowed out to make room for a dull, silver key.

She dug it out and turned it over in her hand. It looked

nothing like the keys her parents used at home, and they owned nothing valuable enough to be locked. Why would her mother hide a key in the back of a travel book?

Slowly, an idea dawned.

Stepping into her slippers and grabbing a lit candle, she tiptoed into the hallway and onto the stairwell, where she climbed to the library.

Inside, the dark blue sky on the ceiling with its golden stars and large moon were the only familiar sights in the now-empty room. The deep quiet of the hollow space was bone chilling. As usual, Avery could feel the slight breeze on her face, but she wasn't here to look at stars tonight.

She had one mission.

She headed straight to the empty bookshelf that revealed the keyhole, thrust the key into the lock, and twisted.

The click was loud as thunder.

With a final glance over her shoulder to be sure she was alone, Avery pushed with all her strength. Slowly she slid the bookcase to the side, and it groaned as if it had been closed a long, long time. She stood at the entry to a long, drafty passageway she guessed would lead into the underbelly of the castle.

Quietly she called out, "Hello?"

Cool air blew through and took out her candle flame with a single whoosh, leaving the room dark as ink.

Voices in the distance seemed to say, *"Go away!"*

But Avery didn't obey.

She knew she had finally discovered the tunnels—the

entrance to the underworld—and with it, the answer to many questions.

Taking a deep breath, she took her first step into the darkness.

about the authors

Trisha White Priebe is a wife, mom, writer, and shameless water polo enthusiast. She advocates for orphans, speaks at retreats, and enjoys assisting her husband in youth ministry. She wrote *Trust, Hope, Pray: Encouragement for the Task of Waiting* and *A Sherlock Holmes Devotional: Uncovering the Mysteries of God.*

Jerry B. Jenkins, former vice president for publishing at Moody Bible Institute of Chicago and currently a member of the board of trustees, is the author of more than 175 books, including the bestselling Left Behind series.

The Ruby Moon

In this exciting sequel to *The Glass Castle*, *The Ruby Moon* opens as preparations begin for the upcoming Olympiads. The castle is buzzing with activity and excitement. Dignitaries are coming. Athletes are training. In a moment of goodwill, the king announces that all members of the kingdom—adults and children alike—will be allowed to attend the Olympiads freely without discrimination. Lucky break or royal trap? Everyone knows the queen is still on the hunt for the king's rightful heir, and kids keep disappearing from the castle. When Avery learns that a male runner is needed for an important race, she volunteers so she can get close to the action. . .but can she hide her true identity? One slip-up could mean a trip to the dungeon—or worse. Much is at stake while the kingdom enjoys the greatest games on earth.